CATHERINE FOSTER

CATHERINE FOSTER

by

H. E. BATES

SEVERN HOUSE PUBLISHERS

This title first published in the U.S.A. 1988 by
SEVERN HOUSE PUBLISHERS INC, New York and
reprinted in Great Britain 1988 by
SEVERN HOUSE PUBLISHERS LTD of
40–42 William IV Street, London WC2N 4DF

British Library Cataloguing in Publication Data
Bates, H. E.
Catherine Foster.
I. Title
823'.912[F]   PR6003.A965
ISBN 0-7278-1608-X

Distributed in the U.S.A. by
Mercedes Distribution Center Inc
62 Imlay Street, Brooklyn, New York 11231

Printed and bound in Great Britain

To
EDWARD GARNETT

PART ONE

COMING out of the porch of the church into the morning sunshine the young wife of Charles Foster, the corn-merchant, did not seem to notice the knot of communicants already gathered there; while they, after casting brief sidelong glances at her, departed across the empty square by twos and threes, dispersing very much like the fragments of some bright shell suddenly dropped, broken and scattered.

Left alone she pensively glanced at the sky, which above the red confusion of roofs resembled faintly some unfinished jigsaw puzzle of blue and milk, and then took the way none of them had taken. This was the pathway by the doctor's garden, where above the red-tiled wall the green spikes of an apricot were showing, and in the crevices of which the petals of some late apple-blossom had lodged in falling and were already fading in the sun. The path skirted the wall like a shadow, winding eastward, leaving the church on her right hand. A concourse of linnets, thrushes, sparrows, blackbirds filled the air with sweet pipings. It was intensely quiet except for their singing in the tall, green-fruited trees and in the sycamores and almonds of the churchyard.

The day was Sunday. The strikers of the clock had been muffled and eight had passed without striking. The streets were still empty; there was no sound, except for the birds, of any life, and the edges of the shadows were softened with dew. The girl, as if not expecting to meet anyone, suddenly took off her hat and fanned her face as she walked along.

The breeze she made moved her abundant hair, black as privet berries, with the neck of her dress and its sleeves. Her dark lashes lowered and rose with it. She breathed it in with long, frequent and delicious sighs.

She walked slower and the church retreated gradually behind a little forest of yews, fruit trees, sycamores and the blood-coloured spears of some gilliflowers rising out of the wall. Now and then she would breathe in the fragrance of the flowers and then hold her breath, as if wishing not to part with whatever sweetness or memory it brought her.

Presently a bend in the path and the wall brought into view a street which, set with two rows of limes, opened on to an open square at the far end. It was empty. The blinds of the houses were down in the sunshine. On the white step of one house a black spaniel had stretched itself and was sleeping.

In that street, in profound quietness and within reach of the church, lived the well-to-do. It was reflected in the green, sleepy shutters of the houses, the haughty windows, the sneering bright knockers on black doors and the circumspect red-and-white sunblinds; and lastly on the brass plates bearing the names of those who lived there. One house belonged to a solicitor, another to a doctor, another to a surveyor. Next door to each other lived a retired draper and a maiden lady. At the far end was a chemist's where, on all days except Sundays, three pear-shaped phials flashed from the window red, emerald and blue. And three doors away stood a bank, in which, on early winter afternoons, when the lights had to be lit, the shadows of the bank-clerks could be seen from three o'clock to five moving across the yellow blinds, discreetly. Between the bank and the retired draper stood the house of Charles Foster, corn-chandler, and the heavy green doors of his yard, the brightly polished yard-bell hanging against the wicket on one side like some heavy ear-ring of gold.

A thrush left the garden to sing in a lime tree. For weeks the weather had been wet and dismal, washing the blossom away. That morning, for the first time, the air was warm, as if at last summer had come.

Abruptly, while crossing from under the wall to the big, green doors, the girl experienced a flood of memory. Her face flushed, and catching sight of herself in the darkness of a window-pane, she saw her manner of approach was quick and flustered.

Then she remembered how, a year before, summer had come with the same exciting suddenness. In the country house where she had lived with her sisters she had woken up one morning to a sky of soft, flowery blue, in an intense hush, and a world of sunlight. In their slanting garden all the birds had begun singing, as on this morning, in a choir together. Tulips had flagged by afternoon, leaving the wallflowers and the lilac to bloom on, mingling proudly their warm, exciting fragrance. The nights had been hot, and afterwards, when rain fell, it was scented with something more delicious and more lovely than even the sunshine had been. She recalled episodes of that summer, details like the dresses she had worn, the playing of some piece of music. She recollected occasions when her husband, then her lover, had come to visit her; appearing suddenly, before she knew of his love, when they were in the garden of an evening or in the summer-house in the afternoon. And always Hester or Charlotte, her sisters, would come running to her and whisper excitedly:

'Charles Foster has come! Charles Foster has come!'

She would go out and greet him. Very shy, and yet at the same time touched and delighted, she would try to maintain, in conversation with him, something between politeness and intimacy. She chose the subjects, if possible, on which she had anything to say. She would talk trivially of flowers, of the weather to be expected, of the best way to clip a yew hedge, ask how soon he thought the black-currants would be ripe, and if he loved the river?

He too had preserved at first a similar attitude towards her. And that attitude, however it had varied, had been towards herself alone. When he arrived, all her sisters, clinging to his arms, dragged him in or out of the house on some pretext, using his Christian name. Only she never touched him, never called him by his name, and never lost her odd, dignified reserve before him.

He was the son of old 'Frenchman' Foster, a magistrate. At school he had not lost a certain preciseness, hardly coldness or reticence, which it seemed to her made him different from all others. He was older than her, though from the first differences had seemed slight. In a quiet way he was handsome, agreeable, considerate and quite attractive. At that time he had been living with his grandfather, learning the corn-merchant's trade in the town, expecting to succeed to the business sooner or later. Sometimes, in the evenings, despite his scrupulous cleanliness, his hands would still smell of dry clover, cattle-cake and grain. But as time went on she came to tolerate these smells and to expect them, just as she tolerated and expected him.

Her courtship had not lasted long. As the days slipped by, before he had spoken to her, she had gone about with the memory of his presence, and as in a dream the secret of which she knew no one could ever betray, had talked to him intimately, touched his face, listened to his voice saying just those things she hoped and longed for him to say. By degrees this presence came to be with her in the first moment after waking and the very last before sleeping. She considered it her duty, as time went on, to devote some part of the day to thinking of him, as at a prayer, in seclusion and alone. She would slip away to some part of the garden cut off by trees and there, watching the smoke of the village sailing across the broad green fields, the sheep grazing and the brook running in and out of its clusters of willow, would surrender herself to him. Near at hand poplars would sigh and the sunshine would seem to come and lie down and seem to sleep by her side. Sometimes the voices of her sisters or of some children would reach her. They did not disturb her, and often for an hour, sometimes for a whole afternoon, that communion of hers would go on. She would look forward to his coming as towards the opening of a flower which slept all day and unfolded only in the evening, and to the time when he would speak as to the time when the flower would drop its modesty and remain open for ever.

By turns she was excited, dreamy, tranquil and profoundly sad. She had always wanted a lover. And this one was so exemplary, careful, considerate and reproachless. Only his vague silences, the way he never showed a longing to be alone with her, and then, when accident had arranged it, suddenly got up and said, 'Your sisters are calling me!' and left her, would make her alternately vexed and melancholy.

Then, just as such spasms seemed to be overpowering

her, he spoke to her. One evening in the garden among the raspberries, a turquoise pendant bearing her name had come unlocked and slipped down among the bushes, and Charles had gone on his knees, crawling about like a child playing as an animal in a jungle, while she had watched him silently. On finding the pendant he had risen quickly, tried hastily to loop it round her neck, and, failing, had given her suddenly one awkward kiss. Blood had rushed to their cheeks, like the colour of the raspberries they had been picking. In a flood of nervous joy she had touched his shoulder. They had gazed at each other with a sort of childish, half-guilty expectancy. From a great distance a bird had set up a prolonged singing. Her heart had beaten time to this with hammer-strokes. Magically, the kiss was repeated. Presently Charlotte, coming into that part of the garden, had seen them, and a minute later all the house had known that Charles was kissing Catherine among the raspberries.

It had been even after all her fears a tenderly exciting wonder. She blushed more often, stole away for longer periods and lay awake at night, listening for something. Soon afterwards Charles's grandfather, the corn-merchant, had died and he had inherited that business as had been expected. She had married him a little later.

Suddenly, under the trees, she paused, put up her fingers to her hair and began retracing her steps. For a moment, she thought, it was too much to expect that she should go beyond those gloomy doors. For some reason she could not go, she had not the courage to face it.

Walking slowly back again, she had even a desire to retreat to some distant spot, green, silent, and lying down there, dream out the day without intrusion. Everywhere, that morning, was so fresh, so warm and tranquil. The limes had not ceased shedding their faint dew. Now she thought, once again, of the garden where she might have stretched serenely hour after hour, as she had so often done, lying with her cheek against the soft vermilion of her Indian shawl, her feet in the grass, her gaze on the sky, and where old Edith, the servant, would come to her, bringing her cold fruit or tea with lemon, talking of her long life, her childhood, in her slow dreaming way.

Suddenly, however, as if realizing the futility of all this, she did return. Retracing her steps, she opened the green wicket and passed into the coolness of the door's heavy shadows, where the blue bricks underfoot were dull with dewiness and where faint spots of moisture gemmed some hart's-tongue ferns and the unpolished finger of a sundial. She detected at once an odour of hay, corn, meal and clover, but tried not to breathe or smell, and then as she advanced, not to see the black wooden barns, sheds and offices at the end of the garden, or the carts with shafts pointing like cannons to the sun.

She lost her air of hesitation. It was as if she thought it expedient to conjure very quickly a change of mood. She swung her hips and arms and bore her head in an easy, stately way that was almost indolent — that way which had already prompted many in that town to think of her as a splendid creature.

SHE belonged to one of those families which spring unexpectedly out of the middle classes but are not claimed by them, very much as certain religious sects throw off dissenters and refuse to acknowledge them though they have the same godhead and may be brothers.

Her family had been a modest, gracious, joyous and above all obscure affair. Obscurity seems to touch every part of such families; their histories, their means, their work, their pastimes. One wonders how they contrive to live in a four-square house with twenty gloomy windows and an enormous, tree-bound garden; how they manage to keep their children at home, educate them and still keep them at home; how they exist, how they spend those slow, silent winter days that are no longer broken by the clap of a bouncing ball or the voice of a bird; what they eat, what friends they have and what they read; why they receive letters bearing stamps from foreign parts, from China, India, or some obscure island of the Archipelago, what creeds they profess, why they are devoted to themselves in a sweet, unalterable, unassailable kind of way which seems their only creed; and where they finally vanish when the house is one day empty, its heavy bolts and locks preserving for ever their obscure mystery.

Her family had been like this. Very secluded and different, its social pretensions were infinitely less than those of the poor, and like a small community governing itself it seemed perfectly happy.

The four sisters were devoted to themselves and to

their mother. Their father had held for ten years some obscure government office in Bombay and had died there, not having made more than half a dozen friends on whom he could rely. There they had lived in a small white bungalow screened off from view by a belt of magnificent palms which the two older girls could vividly remember, coming to England on his death to continue their discreet existence on a meagre pension in the village of his birth. All were dark, olive-skinned, quick-tongued, vivacious creatures. An old school-master had taught them at home, and they kept one servant, named Edith, who could bake old-fashioned wheaten bread and told them stories of her childhood. Growing up they were thought pretty, but serious and unapproachable. One rarely saw them; one wondered always how they lived, if they could love or what they would love. And sometimes when one caught sight of the youngest sister, on some pale autumn afternoon, painting a green bowl of ripe fruit and leaves at an open window, their lives assumed the remote air of some other century.

Catherine, the eldest, had never painted. Instead she played the piano with some beauty and talked of flowers as she might have talked of children.

Such was her devotion to these memories and to her mother that she wrote long letters home every Sunday. She used a writing-tray that her husband had once given her, a ponderous affair in black wood, with three bottles of thick, prismatic glass having silver lids. In form her handwriting was somewhere between round and angular and she wrote quickly, her scheme of punctuation a little wild. From a page of her writing one might have gathered she was ten years younger than she was. She was twenty-five.

On this Sunday afternoon sunshine played unbrokenly over the fresh greenness of the garden. The air was heavy with the scent of spring and all the primroses had not died under the trees. It was a long garden, with uneven rows of apple trees with an odd cherry tree or pear between. Surrounding it was a high red wall, on which plums and a single peach tree flourished beautifully. In the summer masses of blue campanula, anchusa, Sweet St. Johns, pinks and sweet-odoured herbs would spread into a little wilderness.

It was deeply quiet. Somewhere some swallows cried and a thrush tapped a snail on a stone, then sang in a tree, then again tapped and sang. She had written only two lines, when, for some odd reason, she paused and looked up at her husband.

He had fallen asleep, folding his hands across his unbuttoned waistcoat. His shirt and his broad black tie were ruffled. By his side stood a dish of Barcelona nuts, a little pile of broken shells, and a book he had been reading. His breathing was heavy.

She looked at him for a long time and while watching him she thought of what she might have said if she had been made to describe him. It seemed to her that he resembled, most of all, with his black, evenly brushed hair, level-coloured and unexciting features, the hero of some legend in the badly drawn picture-books of her childhood. His eyes were closed, though when opened they were no more restless or challenging. His dark eyebrows arched over them with softness and equanimity, without a trace of displeasure or a frown, having the serenity of some painting intended to flatter. On his lips was a slight pout, as if some dream were troubling him ever so faintly. It gave him a look of being cross, like a child. This made her remember that on her return from communion he had wanted to know:

'Why have you taken off your hat? You haven't walked in the street like it?'

She had replied: 'If I have, what matter?'

'It does matter!'

'There was not a soul about.'

'Still, I should have said it did matter.'

'But if no one saw me?'

'It still matters, you don't know how it lowers respect.'

He had grown silent and sulky. For her part, astounded and hurt, she had tried to assume that dignity which, by treating her as a child, he had half taken away.

Now she reflected the number of times, before her marriage, he must have seen her take off her hat in the sunshine. In the garden, in the woods, walking about the village or the meadows she had never worn one. In the same way he had never reproached her.

By the church three o'clock struck. After the strokes a silence fell, the shrill noise of some swallows fainting away.

Again she began passing through a period of remembrance, reflecting on the first month of her married life, the changes, the disillusionment, the revelation in her husband of such characteristics as strictness in manners and obedience to petty principles, his dislike of music, long walks and flowers, his zeal for business and displaying his knowledge, his stubbornness, his stock thoughts and maxims, and above all the slow, certain acceptance of herself, her love and her happiness as unshakable and unchanging things.

She asked herself if marriage had come to her too

soon, if certain apparently simple yet important adjustments, social, spiritual and physical, should have been made in her courtship. She felt herself fall into despair because they had not been made, regretting the strict preservation of her virginity and ignorance, her obedience to the rules her mother had taught her. What had in those days seemed to her unthinkable and vulgar she now saw as necessary and spiritual. Just as she had never before marriage seen any more of Charles physically than when he gathered gooseberries in his shirt-sleeves, so she had never seen him unreasonable, coarse or ill-tempered. She remembered he used to say: 'If I had a sister, the way I should act before her would be as I act before you.' Now her relations with him were full of the fear of quarrelling, of catastrophe, just as in the first weeks of her married life she had lain awake at night, half in joy, half in terror, wondering if she were to have a child, wondering how she might tell, and how, if it came, she would bear an affliction about which she was still ignorant, unprepared and afraid.

Suddenly, feeling a strange restlessness, she got up and went out. The sunshine was a relief to her. It became suddenly an undreamed-of pleasure to walk along the path under the trees among the dying tulips and jonquils, to hear sounds, to look up through the motionless leaves and see the weathercock on the church standing perfectly still against the blue-enamelled sky.

In those moments she forgot the hushed room where Charles was sleeping, forgot his love-making, his lack of passion and dislike of beauty. Going on she sauntered through the currant bushes, breathing the strong, fragrant smell of their leaves, and pausing, stood under a pear tree, some branches of which hung over the storage-barns and the business offices at the garden's end. The fruit was setting: some had already dropped into the grass beneath and lay with the dead petals.

She thought of a certain pear tree under the window at home. She also thought of that delicate, sensitive first love, melancholy, unreasonable but beautiful, which had begun there. The presence of the other tree would seem at moments to encircle her again with that same tender, moody, naive delight.

There came to her a memory of some summer evening fragrant with jasmine and mown grass from the meadows. A sense of hushed expectancy, broken now and then by a late cuckoo, would give the sense of all nature waiting for a timed happening. The approach of night came in the note of a jay, an early star, a dark cloud. She could see Charles's face as he made love, an unassertive, not highly demonstrative kind of love, and remember the kisses he gave, without desire or passion of any kind, so that it seemed to her like being touched with a brown, dusty moth's wing.

She had been very happy then. Now she frequently felt downcast by the way they sometimes quarrelled, and she grew afraid. She felt something akin to fear even as she stared sideways along the earth and saw a tipped world of tree-boles, dying daffodils and tulips, of black and orange marigolds gazing warmly back at her out of a disordered garden.

For the passionate, vivacious life she had lived with her sisters to be so revolutionized struck her as being quite wrong and unnecessary. And she withdrew like a tender snail and when a voice suddenly called her name:

'Catherine! Catherine!'

She did not answer.

'Where are you? Where have you gone?'

When Charles raised his voice it came through his nose, in a ludicrous, irritating manner.

'Catherine!'

He was searching for her. She could hear the jingle of his watch-chain as he ran.

At last she rose and came forward and met him on a path.

'Mr. and Mrs. Galloway have come,' he explained breathlessly.

She shrank into herself, but without speaking went on.

'I thought for a moment you'd gone off on some mad escapade,' he muttered.

She shuffled her feet in little patches of dying blossoms, as if defying him. She felt she wanted to meet no one. With irritation she dashed some fingers through her hair.

In another moment the two visitors, a fat, self-important little chemist and his wife, with a smart green and crimson parrot's feather in her hat, were beaming foolishly and mouthing flat 'Good afternoons'.

'How nice of you to come,' she answered.

She detested herself for lying and bit her lips while shepherding them towards the porch. And already it seemed boring to have to say 'Shall we have tea?' and to boil the kettle in the stuffy kitchen instead of idling in the sunshine.

Her heart sank as they reached the cool of indoors. Without a word she took away the hats and showed Mrs. Galloway to a bedroom. Mrs. Galloway powdered her greyish flesh with a white puff as big as a sponge. Charles thought her a magnificent-looking woman. Catherine revolted.

But later, over some precious china cups, which her

father had once bought and wherein melted mercifully the hard, dark lines of a world grown solid and real again, she could not help an odd smile. They were so ludicrous when they drank their tea!

'Such a wonderful day!' they would chatter.

'Wonderful!' she agreed. 'Wonderful!'

Her hands moved quickly from cup to cup. In the garden the hidden thrush was still tapping and singing. She cut a lemon, squeezed a half into her tea and ran her juicy fingers across her mouth, tasting their bitterness.

Charles, the chemist and the woman began discussing a case of petty theft at a local jeweller's.

She sat watching the sunshine, profoundly bored by it all.

CHAPTER THREE

ORSE-DEALERS, cattle-dealers, merchants, millers and farmers came in from a radius of ten miles in order to do business with Charles Foster. They arrived very much as they had arrived for the last thirty or forty years of his grandfather's time, in awkward pony-traps, buggies, great pig-carts or milkfloats painted yellow and green and black and splashed with cow-dung; in old, ramshackle cars, by train, and on extraordinary bicycles which enabled them with equal ease to drive flocks of sheep or carry sample bales of straw. They generally came noisily, blusteringly, slamming the great green doors of the yard and tramping through the garden to save time. They drove hard, straight bargains with Charles, tramped back again, shouted genial remarks in the quietness of the garden and swore hard at their ponies, while in his office Charles remained the better off and well-satisfied, and from their constant coming and going derived the comforting sense that these men were his fellows and friends.

In two years he had made many friends. Catherine, on the other hand, had made none. Among his closer friends were Mr. Galloway and Mrs. Galloway who kept the chemist's shop at the street-end and came to see them two nights each week and again on Sunday.

On Sundays, disturbed in writing her weekly letters and often recalling wistfully the tea brought to her by old Edith and set on her soft vermilion shawl beneath a lilac, she managed to entertain them with grave good manners. After pouring tea, she sipped her own slowly, with a ring of lemon, and did not eat much. There

24

would be talk perhaps of baby-linen, medicine and the cost of mutton. Perhaps when tea was done she would play a dance of Chopin or Brahms in order to efface it all. Then they would stare stupidly at her and say:

'How nicely you play! Of course you know the Melody in F?'

She would execute it. In her sensitiveness for music she had a singular pride. Before her marriage she had nearly always played alone or to her mother and sisters before the lamp was alight, with the friendly dusk inspiring and protecting her. When Charles had come she had sometimes been afraid to play. Then, being persuaded at last, she had played more clumsily, she thought, because of that fear and a trembling desire to impress him.

Now she would play only for herself and for brief moments of escape from him and his friends. She would play loudly, to drown their voices, and then softly and ethereally, simply in order to be carried away beyond reach of them, where not even their thoughts could follow.

Forced to return at last she would know then what it meant to be free of them — what it must mean never to have known them. Fears would assail her again, fears that her life, soon, would become also one long conversation on baby-linen, illness, medicine, death and the cost of food; that she might one day lose all her sense for light and freedom, for the beauty of clouds that could be like white butterflies or birds, that with her memories they might slip tired away from her like faded leaves down some endless stream.

Often as she listened to their voices, more especially to Charles's voice, she would long to cry out what she thought of them, and kept silent only because she knew her lips would falter, her breast surge, her eyes grow black with an anger which would mean difficulties, unpleasantness and pain.

When at those rare intervals she became talkative with them it was only to bewilder them or excite their curiosity.

'I have a passion for olives,' she would say, and immediately Galloway would finger his snaky gold watch-chain and wonder at her, not forgetting to say to his Bertha when they were home again:

'Peculiar tastes she has, I think. Well, olives, for instance — where did she cultivate that, I wonder? And why for Lord's sake slop lemons in your tea?'

'Ah! but that's the East, that is,' she would make him understand. 'She was born in the East. Haven't you noticed those native curios dotted about?'

'Those nigger things?'

'Don't say nigger. It's Indian. She'd be very offended.'

'Oh! well, a nigger's a nigger.'

'Still, you're right, it's strange. She's strange.'

'Don't let me see you decking yourself out with a vermilion shawl on Sundays. She may be beautiful, but that spoils her. Today she looked as if her hair had never seen a comb.'

'But she looked so cool at tea.'

'Well, she's odd. Give me Charles. He's sane enough. But don't let me — '

'Oh! get into your night-shirt and don't be silly.'

And they would talk of her in bed.

The trinkets which had excited and puzzled them were pale spice-jars, scraps of native fabric in black and rose, odd fragments of polished coconut or ebony, a tiny Chinese basket of bright straw. Then above the piano she had hung a portrait of her father. His two big, soft Latin eyes gazed down on all comers dreamily. He had been half-Spanish and she was proud that she had taken after him. Upstairs she had hidden away objects which were especially beloved because he had bequeathed them, the red shawl among them, a string of purple beans, a miniature fan with which he had once cooled her fevered head at a party. Each of these had for her its significance, and she thought of them as she thought of trees, flowers, birds.

There were times when she told herself she could not bear to be deprived of these things. This feeling was so strong in her that when she heard one morning the grinding of a saw in the garden and ran out in time to see an old pear tree split and fall across the lawn, she felt herself to be the victim of a tormenting purpose.

'What are you doing?' she shouted.

There was no voice, but only a solemn gathering of leaves high up in the tree to answer this. Two or three figures were moving busily beyond the lawn, gesticulating white sleeves. A saw flashed. From a sturdy brown branch, tipped with loveliest green and tiny russet-coloured pears a rope was hanging. Suddenly this was caught, pulled and gave a sound as loud as a gun-crack in reply.

'But that tree had fruit on, it was full of blossom!' she cried wildly. 'What are you doing?'

She sped across the lawn. Almost at the same moment the tree began falling, like a huge slow hammer, and she found herself confronted in a flash with burial under its great arms. Instinctively she recoiled. A voice warned her, too, and she retreated, the great arc of leaves spending itself and the thin boughs whipping the grass not a foot away.

27

Charles had shouted. Now he rushed to her.

'Don't you know it might have been your death? When you heard me shout you should have kept clear,' he admonished her. He was perspiring and gasping. 'What was the matter with you? What possessed you?'

'Why . . . ?' she stammered. But the words necessary to ask why he had sank down that fruitful young tree would not come to her.

Their old clerk, Hands, doddering about the olive-shaped head of the tree, lifted his yellowish white face and said:

'We wanted more light.'

'More light — more light. What does he mean?' she demanded. 'What does he mean? Did he ask for it to be chopped down? Whose business is it, pray? Who told you to ask? You've been here too long — that's it, we are too ready to give in to you. When you open your mouth anything's done, as if you were master.'

'Catherine! Hold your tongue, hold your tongue!'

But rage shook her. Heedless of Charles she poured out a torrential abuse on the clerk's white head, deriding him, heaping on him a depthless reproach, her heart all curdled to bitterness by the sight of the tree. She could not cease. Her words grew incoherent. Physically she became magnificent, her colour richening, her breasts swelling gloriously under that outrage of pride, under that almost holy contemptuousness springing in reality from a great misery and an inconsolable sense of loss, intensifying every part of her.

'Stop it! I asked for the tree to come down,' cried Charles, grown white. 'Stop it, I say, stop it! How can you say such things?'

She did indeed cease. Resisting Charles's arms, how-

28

ever, she stood gazing down on the tree. Sunshine gave its death a sharpened air of futility. It seemed to claw with soft green nails at the earth, the dying primrose tufts and the white, scarlet and blue-petalled wilderness. Now she saw tiny pears which had been shaken off to the grass, and some yellow bruises on the bark. She stood looking, and then suddenly cried out:

'There's a nest, look, look! It's all broken. But you didn't think of that — no, you didn't think of that!'

Now she spoke softly, with a sort of sad bitterness, her anger abating. No one answered. Hands, turned away, was shaking with a strange paroxysm, as if of tears. 'I hope you're satisfied,' said Charles in a tone which seemed above it all.

Then, as if unaware of his presence she watched a mother thrush that had swooped down. Having flown to where the tree had stood the bird made a trembling hover; presently it circled, blindly, irregularly, with dipping and uncertain wings, as though learning to fly and in a search for something. Then it began screeching, and driven by the vanity of its quest farther into the garden it suddenly perceived the tree and seemed at once caught madly in the throes of maternal distraction, all its instincts pierced to consciousness. As they increased its cries began to speak plainly of profound loss, grief, fright, pain, unhappy bewilderment. Its wings themselves seemed heavy and frantic with sorrow. Each time it approached the nest it veered, swift, baffled, crying. Then joining her the male mingled with hers a distress made more grievous by her own. He too hovered, tore into mad flight, plunged and soared with the same wails of futile grief. Flying together, softly dark and golden, their tilted breasts seemed to strike the sharp pear-boughs as they fell.

29

Impelled by some instinct indefinable to her in that moment Catherine ran among the boughs, her arms stretching upward, as though endeavouring to catch the birds. 'Poor creatures!' she whispered. 'Poor little creatures!'

Over her head the birds kept up their screeching flight. Catherine felt she resembled them in their ineffectual distraction. Then, perceiving some shells of eggs shattered into blue fragments and lodged in the boughs, dripping vivid yolks, she stretched and took some into her hands.

The birds broke into a strange duet of cries. Mortally hurt, she became overcome then with a sense of her own helplessness, the fact that her own unhappy grief, her intelligent and sensitive understanding could avail nothing. She was impotent, impersonal. Brooding over the blue shells frailer than fairy china she suddenly detected hopelessness in all that she had done and said.

But though the birds flew down as if to dispossess her she did not drop the fragments. Within her marvellously responsive instincts of motherhood smouldered pain. She was powerless to utter the emotions she felt. The two thrushes, careering in golden sweeps over the felled tree, expressed it too bitterly and too well.

'Poor creatures!' she could only think. 'Poor little things!'

Hands and Charles had not moved away. As she retraced her way across the lawn she found them in her path. 'Light! They needed light!' she thought. The leaves would make it dark in the offices! — those wretched offices and those lovely leaves of which in the morning there would remain no beauty. If only she had known! But again and again impotency seized her. She could do nothing.

No longer wrathful she walked past Hands and Charles. The clerk's face bore a sered, pale look.

'I hope you are satisfied,' repeated Charles as she passed.

'Heaven!' she flashed in a moment. 'What cause have you to say that again?' It was as if he had blown fierce breaths on a spark, and she drew herself up, trembling.

'What cause? You should be ashamed, I think, talking like that to Hands, who is never well.'

'It's my chest,' whispered the clerk himself. 'It'll be the death of me.' He coughed. 'It gets worse.'

'The way you have upset everyone, it's a disgrace!'

She only glared at him, the enormity of her rage struggling to be free again. Yet what could she say? How explain her attitude?

The birds were still crying and wheeling overhead. The female rested on the high red wall and screeched in discordant and sharp sorrow. Its voice penetrated her, finally severing that link which it seemed had hitherto bound her to Charles, destroying that respect she felt she must dutifully cherish for him, detaching her violently, leaving her in possession of a certain fearlessness, a power to accomplish any kind of defence in the cause of those things she loved, trees, blossoms, clouds — the bereaved thrushes, and if necessary for the cause of another, woman or man, who shared her love of sensuous things.

And prompted by that instinct she flung the light blue fragments of shell into Charles's face as she passed.

CHARLES FOSTER's office was a cramped, narrow little room, washed in white. A single long polished desk, which once in summertime had been dappled with the shadows of pear leaves, now reflected the sky unbrokenly. On the remaining walls a great number of shelves held a little red army of ledgers, the most recent within arm's reach, the faded and obsolete disposed close to the skinning ceiling, undusted and forgotten. Where an area of white appeared some oddment had covered it: a merchant's calendar, a clock, a list of carriers, a cutting from a newspaper which had pleased Charles's fancy. On the desk lay a memorandum of appointments he must keep and notes left for him by Hands the clerk. The door showed a dark half-moon of grease where for countless years Hands's hat had rested.

Some weeks had passed, and Hands's health had broken down. He was an old man and much confinement had seemed to wither him. For a long time he had coughed, at first as if he had a hair in his throat, in an irritated way, then gradually it became a deeper and harsher cough, then it tore at the walls of his chest like some force which must be released, making him its victim. Now a little note had come, saying 'I am ill. I can't get up,' and Charles was forced to remain behind each evening, the gas burning with a faint song above his head and the May twilight deepening gradually from pale to electric blue beyond the window, and busy himself with all the work Hands had left undone. As he worked, writing carefully, adding, subtracting, multiplying, checking over, yellow light fell on his fingers, crept over the desk and over the white paper of his receipts and bills.

Now and then, something, perhaps the thought of Hands, more often the thought of Catherine, would seize him and hold him still, letting him go again only when he lowered his head with fierce determination, a great effort of will, muttering: 'It must be done, no matter what, it must be done.'

With determination he would crouch under the gaslight, reaching out, searching, finding the necessary slip of paper at last, holding it down, checking it. His pen scratched — he liked the pen to scratch, Hands's pen had always scratched. It gave him assurance, it drove away his suspicions of Catherine — of Catherine about Hands, bearing him up and away from the memory of her enraged, unreasonable head shaking itself at that poor, quaking wreck of a man, crying:

'What a fool you are, Hands!'

Much worse, more than he could remember she had cried out too, and all about that old espalier pear tree on the wall, which she declared he had chopped down in a moment of spite for her. The nonsense of it, the aggravating nonsense! And he had no doubt her outburst had had its effect on Hands.

He felt a sudden wave of exasperation rising within himself, but checking it, bent more determinedly over the desk, vowing silently not to think of her. 'Thirteen pounds five and eightpence,' he wrote. 'Ten pounds sixteen and fourpence.' He turned back the pages of the ledger, checked something, went on. Then he saw an entry in his grandfather's writing, a good, round hand, a neat tick to the figures, all revealing to him once more how that old man had understood his work, putting everything on a firm, practical basis which had never wavered, nor had been likely to waver, since. He thought with some pride that he had taken after him; he remembered once hearing someone say of him, 'He has a head level as a ruler,' and had ever since tried to live up to that description, very flattering, doubtless, but probably true. He had never lived in dreams. Often, as now, he thanked God for it. One dream he had certainly had; and it was the dream of Catherine and her sisters, that low garden, the raspberries, the shy, dark smile of greeting for him, the damp hollow when he had for the only time gone on his knees and pressed her hand. Strange, sudden, not quite typical of him, that affair had nevertheless moved him more than perhaps any other thing in his life, and he had married Catherine not so much for love, for talent, for beauty, as out of desire to see the end, for once, of a new experience and so reach emancipation.

Now, without vanishing completely, that memory had grown a little dim. He perceived in himself other virtues — (his finger travelled neatly up and down the index page) — the virtue, above all, of keeping his business straight, steady and profitable. Other people, he granted — his wife among them — might have some special virtue too. Catherine, for instance, played the piano well. Galloway could mix a prescription. Old Hands's wife made lace. But none of them could say, as he did, that that peculiar virtue was the heart of his life, without which he would have sickened, grown quite wretched and probably have died.

He went on writing, the file now and then squeaking and clicking, the tissues rustling, the pen always scratching. Suddenly some figures confused him. He wrestled with them and then, surrendering, took the papers into the house and said:

'Come and help me with the accounts. Leave playing for now.'

She was sitting playing, her back to the lamp-light. Half-turning she begged:

'No, no, don't ask me. I don't understand figures. They're Greek to me.'

'But what is it?' he asked, spreading out his plump fingers, 'it's nothing. I don't want you to add up anything. Read out the figures and I'll check them from another list, that's all.'

Leaving the piano she sat down by him, obeying his abrupt, 'Bring the lamp with you,' with a timidity which astonished her. Extending her hands with meekness for the papers he pushed across, she seemed to slip suddenly back into the depths of her childhood, when she had been taught to obey with calmness and readiness every commanding voice. She arranged the papers he gave her, waited till he said, 'Ready, check each item,' and then lowered her eyes. A brief, cold silence took place before he spoke. His dry, calculating cough and the smell coming from him of old straw, seed and meal jarred and depressed her. And as if afraid of giving way to one emotion or the other she began slowly twining about her long right forefinger a ringlet of her black hair.

'January fifteen, thirty-four pounds six and eightpence,' he read to her. 'February nine, twenty-eight pounds ten shillings; February twenty-three, eighteen pounds six and a penny; March fourteen, nine pounds seventeen and seven. . . .'

Absentmindedly she once glanced up, not caring if the items were right or wrong, and watched him. His face became the calm, affable symbol of something she vaguely hated. His plump cheeks and lips seemed to be

35

moving in a perpetual argument on some point which did not matter. Alternately it bored and infuriated her. Fragments of items swept through her brain in a meaningless horde.

When she calmed again she fell under the spell of his persistent voice. Mechanically she nodded, turned over the leaves, rectified mistakes. She conceived him in calmness to be what he was — the dry, reasoned figure of business who in turn conceived her as an institution, a cypher, a slave to a dreary domesticity. She saw him as a being necessarily in authority over some person or thing, a man who nevertheless made friends by his affability and his readiness to listen to some fresh opinion of things while not changing in the faintest degree his own.

'I am progressive, I like something to happen,' he would declare. He voted Liberal and in the autumn went shooting. He was liked for his calm, good-natured acceptance of things, his easy morality, his ability to enjoy a joke and kill with both barrels. And in his zeal to show what he thought of her before his friends he had once spoken of music as the Divine gift from God.

His behaviour towards her was sometimes of an extraordinary kind. Half-tolerant, half-patronizing, he reproved her at inconceivable moments and used to laugh a very low, rasping laugh at the solemn expression of dreaminess with which he sometimes caught her looking into space. She hated this laugh, hated the plump, dancing fleshiness of his face, the monstrous inanity of it all, the soullessness. His reproofs, his stupidity, his conventions, his easy morality she could endure, but not this laugh, from the depth of which there rang an incredibly hard note, harsh and metallic to her as the rasping of some cheap toy.

36

She in turn did extraordinary things to defend herself. In bed at night, very soft, low sounds, as if of stirring boughs or grass, crept about her and seemed to play in an endless dancing colonnade about her face. They brought her deep peacefulness in which she revelled with delight. Suddenly a recollection of that laugh would come, insistent and impotent, shocking her. She would struggle, lie inert, meet it with desperation, with subtlety. But again and again it defeated her and she caught its uncanny echo in the stillness, the cries of bats, the moving boughs and leaves, and the toy thunder of moths struggling frantically against the glass withholding from them the freedom of the warm, dark, beckoning night.

She sprinkled scent in the bosom of her dresses. It revived in her some vague memory of the past, filling her with the extraordinarily calm, sure fortitude she gained sometimes from a touch with beauty, a remembrance of Indian hills, a flaunting palm against the brilliance of the unalterably blue sky.

That night, by the faintest bend of her head she could breathe fragrance as she sat at that table reciting the details of the dreariest accounts in all the world. She could breathe extravagantly of it, slowly, ecstatically, as if accepting the prolonged caress of a lover. Her fears of him vanished, all the things set there to frighten and dismay. His drab, monotonous voice was borne away as if the wind had suddenly turned. It seemed to her a resource on which she might rely for ever, until suddenly inclining his head to ask: 'Is it ten pounds six and eight, or six and three?' he caught an overpowering breath of verbena and recoiled, saying:

'What's that you've got on? What is it? Verbena? You smell like a scent-shop. How cheap!'

It was the end. He seemed to her suddenly a heap of dry bones, not a man. A sort of cold inaction seized her. She stood looking at the lamp with eyes dark and sombre, as if bruised. Then she flung on her heel and rushed into the darkness of the stairs as to a sanctuary.

Step by step she was followed by that preposterous laugh of his, silly, rattling and prolonged, as if he were truly appreciative of her tears.

IT came to the time of meadow-sweet and campion, and the meadows where Catherine so often wandered were vital with scent and over-crept with pretty ground creatures, running cranesbill, speedwell and yellow vetch, with heads of stiff, glazed buttercups and mauve lady-smocks never still above the grasses. The doddle-willows shook off the last of their faded gold tassels to the sunny river and covered themselves with a mature, silver green. Cuckoos in ash trees, meadow-pippits and willow-wrens from one never knew where, a corn-crake at night, all came in with a surprise of notes; the blackbird sang more thrillingly; the owl called in a mischievous, jolly way, and on the fringes of woods one heard the sweetest, sleepiest of voices, and with the sound of the doves all the earth moved half-consciously into summer.

After returning one day from wandering along the river-side, she found a letter from her mother. Her wild bouquet of lady-smocks, bull-daisies and pale orchis was thrown into a chair, and lying back on the sofa she read with all the joyful satisfaction of some hope long cherished and realized at last. Her mother was coming and bringing Charlotte. It was at first too sweet to believe, and then too intimately sweet ever to discredit again, and life assumed a new aspect and tone as she thought of them.

The days were broken by endless plans of what they should do, what she should say to them, how into two days could be crowded all the little absurd events and memories she had preserved for them.

Loneliness disappeared — she wondered how it had ever existed, or could have burdened her. Miraculously the indifference of Charles, the disappointment about the pear tree and the worry about Hands's illness slipped away, too, and she began to live in a kind of protracted dream, apart from them.

The day of their arrival was splendid, the sky a gown of blue with faint embroideries of white cloud. Even so early as seven o'clock a bee droned in at the window and swam from bowl to bowl, summer in its very sound.

She was awake and up, running about in her slippers. There were countless things to do, and all of them to her wonderful. All morning she spent making salad in dishes of quaint pottery, skinning almonds, folding her table-napkins like bishops' mitres, garnishing and flavouring, and towards noon she was running up and down to the rooms which they would occupy, packing away the camphor-balls in a lace bag and leaving in their places sprays of fresh lavender, like tiny sheaves of blue barley.

These moments of her life were half-poetic. Within her lay an intense resource of something not merely sweet and tender, but burning and passionate, half-tempestuous when it struggled to escape from her.

She took a little pony-trap Charles kept for business when she went to the station. Charles liked a horse and would even have hunted had he possessed the necessary social prestige and money, and of course a horse cost him nothing to fodder. The pony's name was Bill, and his driver would have to keep up a constant 'Bill, Bill, Bill!' to make him go.

High up in the trap she caught sight of the river. In the drowsy morning sunlight miles of green meadows seemed to be holding it between them with a sense of secure peacefulness, and it was empty, except for a barge passing a lock ten fields upstream. To hire a punt and drift languorously far away, past little towns and villages on the banks, and boil tea under a stooping willow with a fire of twigs and grass, seemed to her suddenly a perfect adventure. Every moment to the station she thought it an increasingly splendid idea. She even felt impatient as she watched the slow ball of train smoke unwinding itself like swansdown far away.

The meeting was very exciting. They kissed each other twice. The green of Charlotte's dress gleamed like the scales of a fish in the sunshine; she too was gay and dark.

They had to squeeze against each other before there was room in the trap. Catherine drove again. Twenty years before her mother would have worn a bustle, a high lace collar kept in place with strips of whalebone, and perhaps a watch of blue enamel and gold, the very latest thing, pinned on her silk blouse. She had never quite lost the impression of this and she sat very upright, though not stiff, as they drove along.

'Bill, Bill!' cried Catherine repeatedly. 'We're going on the river.'

'Oh! when, when?'

'This afternoon. Look!' She pointed with her whip to the green, flat meadows. 'Bill, Bill!' The sun beamed down on three happy, averted faces. 'It will be quiet down there and we can take tea.'

'A boat?' asked Charlotte.

'A punt. We shall drift. Bill, Bill!'

The pony jibbed at a white dog, set them all bumping like sacks against each other and Catherine kept up her 'Bill, Bill, Bill!' more shrilly than ever.

All three burst out laughing, and while they bumped

along she, with little catches of breath and strange swellings of her bosom, told them how happy she was and how delightedly she had planned everything and waited for their coming. Also she forgot Hands, the chemist, her misery at her lack of friends, until nothing of the old life seemed to remain.

She flourished the whip and Bill bore them at a stately gallop into the cool dappling light under the arch of limes.

Charles was standing at the door, ready to greet them. He looked stupid against their rollicking gaiety.

'Charles, Charles!' she began to call in the most excited voice: 'Charles! — whoa, Bill, whoa! — Charles, we're going on the river, we're going on the river!'

Bill stopped, the harness tinkled like silvery bells as she jumped down amid more laughter. She waltzed about, and the shadowy look flashing over Charles's face was lost on her.

THAT afternoon she stood at the foot of the stairs, calling Charlotte's name, pleading 'Shall you ever be ready?', with the red shawl her mother had given her slung over her arm, telling herself she would slip it across her shoulders as she lay back in the punt, and afterwards, on the grass under the willow, set out the tea on it, as old Edith used to do. She looked happy and reflected that even though she had wished for it, prayed and struggled as for nothing else, happiness had today come to her with a fullness all unexpected and un-dreamed.

A basket with plates, kettle and cups stood in the hall. In another on the table she had packed cherry-tarts, cucumber, lettuces, the bread her mother had brought and some cakes with cinnamon. She carried a sunshade of yellow and green.

Outside Charles was walking about the garden, in a grey tweed suit, with her mother, pointing to the trees. Watching him, observing his contentment, she was glad, half-thinking that this was the turning-point, that for ever afterwards some ripple of the extraordinary happiness of this day would run gently across their lives, disturbing them into some unexpected act of grace, of light, of magnanimity towards each other.

Presently Charlotte ran downstairs with her white hat in her hands and they went into the garden to call Charles and her mother. Going out under the limes, the sun dappling their faces, Charles and her mother first, Charlotte and herself following, they called back-wards and forwards to each other with high-pitched

43

voices, resembling for all the world a party of ingenuous children off for a tea-party.

The bank on which the boat-house stood was steep, the white, wooden house surrounded by willows and chestnuts leaning thirstily to water's edge. Boats were pulled high up under the shade, where also were little green tables set out for tea. As they arrived a crew of rowers in light slips ran out of the boat-house with their boat, set it on the water and skimmed away.

Seeing them, Charles must begin suddenly insisting like a boy: 'I want a boat — do let's take a boat!' while they beseeched him, 'It's not safe, you can't row,' clinging to his arms, entreating him not to be so silly, saying it was a punt they wanted, not a boat, and a punt they must have. 'Charles! don't be absurd!' He folded his arms across his chest, mocking for a moment, his wrists lying on his fore-arms, thin and white. Then suddenly, in his dry unprotesting way, he gave into them, his arms falling to his side and his faint smile, as if he had never wanted either to punt or row, fading away into something dry and chilling in its resignation. And in another moment or two they were getting into a punt, Charlotte side by side with her mother, Catherine spreading out the intense vermilion of the shawl and covering it with her cool-looking limbs, and the boat-house keeper giving them a gentle push away.

In the serene, warm air of that afternoon, the summer current of the river moving slowly, they hardly drifted at all. Now and then Charles, silent, pitifully ludicrous in his stiff collar and thick tweed, would stand up and thrust down the punt-pole through the long green weeds, and the women would observe how serenely they were borne along, their hands rippling the water, their faces turned alternately to the meadows or the

44

blue sky, now and then remarking: 'How green the reeds are! I saw a fish just then — a flattish one, with spots on. What would it be?' and uttering at intervals playful screams when Charles splashed them and the punt and himself with cool, silver bows of water.

As she lay still, her eyes open, watching the sky and the willows from that strange angle in the punt's bottom, the sky more spacious, more intense, and the trees growing upside down in the stream, she felt restful, happy that there had been no hitch in it all, glad of the intenseness of life bearing upon her, breathing it in with long delicious breaths and flutters of joy. All recollections of the past she threw off with a kind of nervous haste. Once only, happening to glance up and catching sight of the pale, dull expression of weariness on Charles's face, a disquieting reproachfulness seized her, and suddenly extending her arms upward, she seized his, stopped them, and said:

'Don't punt any more.'

'Why, would you like to try?' he asked.

'Rest a little.'

'No use. Come, it's easy. You have a try.'

'No, let's drift,' she urged, 'and come down and sit with me.'

He drew the pole from the water and would in another moment have sat down by her, for she was making room on the shawl, when Charlotte half-screamed: 'A kingfisher!' making them follow the brilliant passage of the bird, a long electric spark in the sunshine, until it disappeared among the shadowy greenness far ahead. For some reason, after that, though the red space of the shawl remained deserted, she did not think of asking him to sit down again, but as if feeling the heat, put up her sunshade, while he stood motionless behind, not punting, as if in his dry, expressionless way feeling the pain of it all.

Soon afterwards, when they glided in under the willows, they found a cool, still, splendid place. The earth gave up the sound of bees and grasshoppers with a live, murmurous air. Across the green lakes of grass beyond the river a meadow-crake sent harsh, resentful calls, between which seemed to come down an intense, waiting silence. The women walked about stretching their legs like three bright, stiff dolls among the green.

Charlotte and Catherine departed to gather wood. Under the trees their voices echoed, ringing. Spreading out the shawl their mother sat down, fanning herself, while presently at her side, after feeling if the grass was damp, Charles plumped down also, undid his waistcoat, stretched himself and closed his eyes. But not a moment seemed to pass before Catherine, coming back again, dangled some pale, faintly scented flowers into his face, making him sit up with a fierce spluttering jerk, resenting her pale face above the flowers, laughing at him. And feeling as if about to sneeze he glowered at her:

'Isn't that rather silly when I'm lying on my back?' But she took no notice of him.

'Think what you're doing. I might have choked.'

But she was over beside the bank, sorting out the eatables, saying nothing for fear of unpleasantness before Charlotte and her mother, feeling angry with him, wishing for a moment he had not come. To her scenes were mean and detestable, and that day, most of all, she longed to have not an unpleasant moment or word.

Charles, while she arranged for tea, lighted a fire. Presently, liking the smell of the grey wood-smoke

46

which crept up through the trees, she forgot what had passed, and when they sat down on the bank, the rest languid and quiet, she laughed and sowed crumbs on the water.

'Why do you keep doing that?' asked Charles.

'I'm happy, that's all! I'm happy!'

He replied nothing, but she understood by his silence, his way of staring across the meadows and gulping his food that he thought her wasteful, childish and possibly absurd. She lay down, full length, and stared at the sky. But little by little, watching the light clouds, the blueness, the willows, the reeds and a string of birds all making by their reflections another world in the water, her sense of uneasiness and injury passed again.

As they sat there other boats passed up and down the river, people waving their hands, while they waved back again. In one boat a gramophone played some slow, sentimental air and a man sat singing, wearing a ridiculous check shirt with white trousers, looking foolishly happy and singing louder as he passed, while Catherine watched him and the boat dropping down the stream, thinking that there was something lovable, haunting and sweet about it all, about the melody, his strange appearance, the ripples, the sound of his voice drifting back over the water. And feeling restful, at peace, she looked at Charles with a faint smile.

But the next moment, filled suddenly with unexpected gaiety, she got up and cried:

'Let's go into the woods!'

'Why go into the woods?' repeated Charles. 'It's very nice here. Why go away?'

'Come, don't be lazy!'

'But it's pleasant here. It's nice. Why go away? What for?'

She stood there not knowing whether to be angry or to leave him without a word. And then he said:

'Go if you want to go. I don't object. Go if you want to go.'

She went.

It was shadowy in the woods, of a shadowiness cool and refreshing, in which woodpeckers kept laughing high up in the branches and there was a smell of honeysuckle and alder. She held out her hands, let the leaves touch her fingers as they passed, and slowly, yet overwhelmed completely, let her sense of unblemished happiness return. And for a long time they remained there, gathering handfuls of honeysuckle and dog-rose, sometimes in silence, sometimes talking in high-pitched voices, sometimes with the sound of wood-doves and the voices of boating-parties reaching them from far away.

When they returned she was at a pinnacle of happiness, calling Charles's name long before they reached him, entreating him at last:

'Have we been long? Were you lonely? Why didn't you come?'

And it seemed to her at that moment that if he had looked up and said, 'It's all right: in my way I'm happy enough,' she would have understood and would have pressed his hand, so that he would have known. But he remarked at once:

'It gets chilly. What time is it? Oughtn't we to go?'

It was past seven o'clock. Yes, perhaps they ought to go. They began to return. In the punt he stood staring straight ahead of him, as if everything — the punt, the river, the flowers, the way Charlotte sometimes burst out laughing — bored him to a point of melancholy.

To her the evening sunshine, the ripples on the water,

the silence, the slow motion of the punt and the scent of honeysuckle lying in her lap were enchanting. She noticed nothing of him. Later, in the house, at supper and when they were undressing for bed, it even seemed to her that he had caught some of the richness of that day's happiness, too.

But suddenly he complainingly muttered: 'They charged me five-and-six for that boat. Five-and-six! I complained, but what's the use of talking to them?'

She lay still, staring, aghast. She could say nothing. And over and over again, as she lay there, she could only think of those words, 'They charged me five-and-sixpence for the boat,' and of what they meant to her. And it seemed to her suddenly that she had slipped hopelessly back into the uneventfulness, the pettiness and weariness of her former life, that everything she had done and seen on the river, everything, the kingfisher, the shadows on the stream, the twilight, the hum of bees, the thyme and the tea-party on the bank amounted to nothing. She hated Charles over and over again for his meanness and soullessness. She hated him! At last, unable to bear it any longer, she seized the sheet, pulled it over her face and tried to weep. Nothing came, not a sound. Her throat seemed parched and hot, her fingers restless, as if to seize something. She threw off the coverlet, and lay utterly still, staring at the ceiling. She ached and her forehead burned. But little by little first her arms, then her hands, face, neck and chest grew cold. Presently she began to shiver. At last, chill and unhappy, she drew herself down, covered her face again, crept close to Charles, and with the misery and irony of her position seizing her suddenly lay bitterly muttering over and over again, under her breath:

'Oh! God! Oh! God!'

PART TWO

THE only other member of the family of Fosters, besides old Frenchman, the magistrate, and Annie his wife, was a younger son, whose name was Andrew. His history, flavoured by a startling incident in his twenty-second year, had given him a faintly notorious prestige he never deserved. There were people who knew and discussed him long after the steady and amenable Charles had passed into the curious oblivion of business and marriage, slandering him, condemning him, blackening him and duly horrified by his mode of life. There were others, and among them a distinct proportion of women, who felt very much the reverse of all this and excused him, defended him and even professed affection in spite of everything. One reason for both sorts of opinion was that he possessed enviable good looks, insinuating and charming manners and the invaluable but often fatal capacity to invoke good confidence. A second was that he had once become a father at a disarmingly early age, though his paternity had abruptly ceased after the fifth day, owing to neglect by the girlish mother. Lastly, apprenticed by his father to a deaf and trustworthy old architect, he had been accused of swindling a little money.

This episode had been at once hushed up, though for some reason it was openly discussed and commented on, just as if he had been brought before the local magistrate like another. His father had refunded the money, and acting like the father in the parable of the prodigal, had given him the two hundred and fifty pounds legacy from his grandfather and sent him away. The boy vowed he would never come back, acted as if he had done something righteous but unappreciated, and went to Germany.

He chose Germany for one reason. This was a love of music, which none of his family shared. And after making friendships in London with a party of young people about to go over for a large musical festival, he accompanied them gladly. There he found life truly agreeable in his own way, for wine was cheap and plentiful; cafés were not devitalized by an occupation of French and English soldiers; music was ardently played in every town, and on the Rhine, among the summer vineyards and orchards, and in the dark, sweet-smelling forest of birches and pines he could feel as if he were living a deep, free, idyllic life. He stayed there until the following spring. By that time he knew how many glasses of Rhenish wine it took to make him drunk; he could sing 'Deutschland, Deutschland!' freely with the peasants; and he had loved, ardently and successfully, five or six quite beautiful women.

It was early summer when he returned to England. Blackbirds were in full song in the green trees, there were sweet, familiar English scents and the corn was still like grass, still far from having ears. How fresh, blue, and warm the sky was each morning!

But after a time he grew bored doing nothing. His money was dwindling, too, and finally he went and found work with some architects in Harkloe, ten miles from his brother.

Not many weeks later he was seized with a kind of impish desire to call on Charles, and very soon afterwards, one Sunday, did so. The sound of a Chopin mazurka being tolerably well played greeted him as he knocked at the big black door of the house. Coming out of the warm, thunderous silence of that Sunday afternoon, its gay, silver notes were unexpected and startled him. A moment later he was startled, too, by the fluttering appearance of Catherine, whom he had half forgotten, in a thin, pale, floating sort of dress, and by her soft, contralto voice saying:

'Charles is not at home, but you will come in, won't you?'

There was a thunderstorm brooding. The sky was dark and seemed to hang low, as if waiting to touch the tips of the limes and the chestnut blossoms, standing stiff and waxen like unlit candles among their bright, flagged leaves.

Catherine herself felt nervous, especially when he said suddenly:

'I think you play rather beautifully.'

She knew nothing of him. His notorious escapade had never, for obvious reasons, been discussed in her family or between her and Charles. She was nervous also because of the thunderstorm and continually forgot the last remark he made. Now and then she was aware of his appraising watch on her.

She sat still, her hands together. The storm, every moment nearer and more menacing, set the sky moving slowly across from west to east, like some dark slide, it seemed to her, being inserted for a photograph. Alternately watching it and the face before her, she had a feeling of apprehension, half-wishing he would go. But he sat on. Then unexpectedly there sprang out a flash in which the trees, the roofs, the objects in the room seemed to sicken with pale light, and their two faces sprang into a strange brightness, still sepulchral and unreal, filling her with the odd idea, as she sat there breathlessly waiting for the thunder to come, that their photographs must actually have been taken, vivid and faithful, on the dark, yellowish glass of the sky. For a second or two she even sat reflecting on what they must have looked like, she frightened and wild, he sensuous, mournful, not at ease, as if having slipped into the picture by mistake.

Everything seemed peculiar and unreal. She was not accustomed to anything, as if in a strange house.

Presently the thunder broke. She uttered a little 'Oh!' and stopped her ears, while he was silent. Then little by little the thunder rolled off and quietness came again. After that she sat waiting for him to speak.

But he said nothing. Restless and unnerved she got up and went and stood by the window. She thought how still it all was. Looking up, beyond the still, blackish leaves, she longed more than ever for rain to fall, to hear the warm, passionate swish of it sweeping through the leaves, for the coolness and relief of it. She stood softly rubbing her fingers over her pale cheeks, as though they were of china and she were polishing them.

She wore a look of perplexity. She wondered how long Charles would be, dreamed a little. Suddenly it occurred to her to turn and say:

'What do you do nowadays?'

He had apparently been dreaming too and looked startled before answering:

'I have work in Harkloe. I saw your sisters there a week ago.'

'My sisters!' she exclaimed.

'Yes. It was market-day. They were shopping.'

'Yes, yes?' She grew excited. Her eyes brightened. 'All three sisters?'

'Only Charlotte and Hester.'

'What dress had Charlotte on? A green one? Do you remember?'

'No, I don't remember!'

'Did they see you?'

'No, I caught sight of them from my office-window, that's all.'

Suddenly talk became imperatively necessary to her. She chattered heedlessly.

So he had seen her sisters? That meant so much to her. And did he live absolutely at Harkloe, he had a room there? Were the shops nice still? She had not been there for perhaps six months, when she had bought five yards of silk, turquoise colour, very expensive, and there had been a row about it. She asked many questions. He was attentive, patient, his eyes on some sprays of lilac she had left on the table, an air about him as if he liked it all — her voice, the scent, the half-dark room, the still, stormy sky. It grew darker, though rain still did not come, only now and again thunder bringing a strange, trembling silence while they waited on.

Then quite suddenly rain came falling with a loud murmur, sweeping fiercely up against the panes after its long dull roar through the bushes and trees. To her it was like being near the sea, in a storm, with the spray flying. The sense of overpowering sultriness passed, filling her suddenly with a sense of cool, blessed relief, making her recline backwards, languorously flinging out her arms with a sigh:

'God! how delicious!'

He said nothing. The rain fell heavier, louder, fiercer, and then, after a moment or two, there was a fragrance with it. She caught it and flinging out her arms repeated:

'Delicious! Isn't it delicious?'

57

For a while she listened intently to its fall on the roofs, the earth, the branches and thick leaves. She heard it beating on some leaves of rhubarb as if on a drum. Then she inquired of him suddenly:

'Tell me what goes on at Harkloe now.'

'What do you mean — the life?' he asked.

'Yes.'

'It's no different.'

What did he mean by that? she asked herself. Was he, too, dissatisfied?

'Ah, no,' she went on, 'the theatres — the dances — that kind of thing.'

'There's not much.'

'But there's something. Music, for instance?' she suggested. 'There's music?'

What did he say? He mumbled so. The Salvation Army? — Elijah?

Then suddenly he burst out, remembering in a flash and with a strange, trembling enthusiasm, the details of some recital of Chopin he had seen — all Chopin, by someone whose name he could not remember, a pianist — God! no, the name would not come — but it was Chopin, entirely Chopin — Chopin for one whole afternoon, in the hall there, one Sunday. Yes, soon! It was true, and he had almost forgotten to tell her! She, of course, loved Chopin? — him, above all? And the Prelude where one note went on and on, tapping and falling, as someone had said, like dripping rain on a summer's night — perhaps such a storm as this — possibly? — she loved that too?

His wide, rather sensual-looking lips moved swiftly when he spoke. With intense surprise and delight she got up and looked at him. It was evident to her he was moved, that he meant it all.

58

'Shall you go?' she asked, in a half-whisper.

'Yes.'

'I shall think of you,' she said.

Would he understand that? she asked herself, would he understand that she also longed, passionately, now he had told her, for that afternoon, to go out of reach of the Galloways, their eternal tea and their chatter, and listen to that recital, above all to that Prelude which she also lived with passion and delight?

She sat down. She was trembling. Then she began to play, not speaking. The first notes came, passed, seemed to ally themselves with the wet dripping gloominess beyond, evoking for her endless and miraculous memories. She heard him sigh, 'That's the Prelude,' and then sink into silence.

'God! If only I could go!' she thought.

The thought ran through her playing, like the dropping note.

She finished the prelude, swung round on the stool and sat looking at him. His eyes were in a fixed, meditative gaze. And looking at him it seemed that he was about to say something, something fervent and exciting, perhaps to thank her, to praise her, to invite her to go with him to that recital. His expression seemed to her intense, pathetic, as though he were struggling with something, as though he longed to express himself. Yet he said nothing, and she, not understanding, not sure of herself, remained silent also, and at last, getting up, moved silently away.

Five minutes later Charles returned from visiting Hands, who was growing worse. He greeted his brother simply through sheer astonishment. A look of outrage and confusion, which gave him a hot colour, was succeeded by a struggle to look dignified and indignant.

He turned pale suddenly, flourished a careless-looking handkerchief, glanced at his watch, said it was later than he thought it would be, plucked the petal of a fox-glove in a jar, and tearing it slowly to fragments, lapsed into a chilly tolerance, not speaking.

His brother became reserved also, his eyes on the purple storm and the rain. Catherine, utterly ignorant of the cause of that attitude, ran upstairs to change her dress, very happy in the thought of listening to Chopin played by a great master.

CHAPTER TWO

THOUGH he had said nothing, the conviction never left her from that moment that he would expect her at that concert, and a fortnight later she took the Sunday afternoon train to Harkloe. Over everything lay a sleepy brightness; a bluebottle droned in the carriage window. The train jolted and stopped persistently, giving her long, dreary glimpses of fields with dry ponds, stunted trees and telegraph poles, depressing to her even in sunlight. Sometimes she shut her eyes and obliterated them.

In the same way she dismissed Charles as a figure who had with an ironic blandness said:

'I don't see why you want to go, but go if you want to go, I shan't bother. Perhaps Andrew will be there and you can sit with him.'

As the train drew on, transporting her gradually from an uneventful past, she thought of the concert, the crowded hall and the thrill of listening. Occasionally growing hot with excitement she leaned from the window and watched for the roofs and spires of the town to come. A cool wind refreshed her face and teased her breast. All the time she would say to herself:

'Make the most of it, every moment, every moment. It may not happen again.'

The train drew in at last. It was late and she hurried from the station. Outside the hall one or two people were lingering at the doors. Afraid of missing even a moment of that pleasure she had so long looked forward to she entered at once, running up the steps without pausing. Then at the doors a voice suddenly entreated her:

'Hush, madam, they have begun.'

She stood still, disappointed, bewildered. Presently she woke, gradually, to the sound of notes reaching her softly as if from far away, and she listened intently. It was the Prelude in A, which she recognized, but which seemed to her different, more inspiring in its sweet beauty. When it had finished she sat down in her seat, with a sort of meditative joy. Buying a programme absently, she glanced at it and let it fall to her lap unread. The hall was crowded. She had never been there before, and now, glancing up at the heavily moulded roof with its nymphs and cherubs, vine and myrtle wreaths about the pillars, and the portraits of all the town-councillors since Victorian days, she had a feeling of being in some important place. It was not restful, not even unusual or beautiful, but with the sun slanting across it from the high, coloured windows, warming it, caressing the heads of the audience, it added in some way to her experience, her intense joy. She seemed to be living on a higher plane, as she had done when seeing her mother.

Presently, when the pianist returned to the platform, she took in everything — the bowing, the elaborate gestures, the applause, the waiting, the tiresome whispers, the sudden shadow across the piano, the first notes. Then, in a sort of dream, she listened to one piece after another. Her manner became intense, almost religious. And she would think: Is there in life anything more wonderful than this? She gripped her hands, picked the fingers of her gloves, took off her gloves and touched her cheeks with her hands — things she did absently and feebly, as if to reveal how low the practical, objective life in her had ebbed, giving way to the dreamy, imaginative side of her that had slept so long.

The playing was remarkable; and somehow, that day, the pieces she knew and admired most had been chosen. It affected her so much that she sat as if under the influence of some intoxicant, staring straight before her, her intensity never lessening.

When the interval arrived she became aware of someone trying to attract her attention. She felt uneasy, looked this way and that, and then saw someone raise a hand. And in a moment Andrew came to her, stood by her seat and began talking.

He said at once: 'I thought I should see you.' Then later, after they had stood in silence a moment or two, he suddenly remarked:

'You look paler — and a little thinner. Haven't you been well?'

She only replied: 'It's nothing. Sometimes I don't sleep well, that's all.'

'I'm sorry,' he said.

He spoke softly, kindly and with sympathy. Suddenly it seemed to her that for a long time she had needed someone with just such care and understanding to talk to her. The thought increased in her that she was glad to be with him.

Presently he said: 'You see they are going to play the Prelude?' and looked at her intently.

'Which Prelude?' she asked, faintly shaking her head.

'You remember you played it the night it thundered and I came to see you.'

'Ah! yes. I saw that — I'm glad.'

The next moment he asked her to get up and walk about with him, and she did so. As they walked up and down in the vestibule, mingling with other people, discussing the performance, her sense of uneasiness returned. But she said nothing. Presently they went on discussing music, the pianist and above all, Chopin. She talked a little faster (he noted in that moment how colour returned to her face), using words fresh to her, conscious, now and then, of some new manner of thought.

And then he asked:

'Is anyone with you?'

'No, I'm alone.'

'So Charles didn't come?'

'He sleeps on Sundays.'

She had not meant to be malicious or ironical, only perhaps mischievous in telling what was, after all, the truth; but she laughed when speaking, evoking a response in his face so immediate, so unexpected, and so faithful that it was as if she had said: 'Laugh at him when I tell you to.'

A little uneasy again, she changed the subject, telling him of her arrival, and the Prelude in A, of the effect of its half-sad, half-joyous sweetness on her.

Then as they walked slowly back he remarked, with fervour: 'I have always loved that Prelude.'

Now it seemed to her that he was moved, genuinely, from some force within himself and not from something she had said. He did not go back to his seat but stood beside her. And during those moments, while waiting for the concert to go on, she sat watching him, studying his face. He was not aware of it, having slipped into a kind of reverie, and staring at the blue curtains, seemed to her dominated by some thought, compelling and problematic. His head slightly lowered, his eyes perfectly still, it was as if the memory of something were filling him with uneasy joy, with some ecstasy, like her own, almost impossible to bear.

64

He unsettled her and she longed for the performance to go on. She waited, a little impatient. Then the pianist came back; it was all about to begin again, and she was listening with more intensity, with a quieter, deeper joy, as if all that had gone before had been only a rehearsal. She leaned back, shut her eyes and gave herself up to emotion.

In one of the intervals Andrew bent down and observed: 'The Prelude is next.' She started. He seemed so near, and she had forgotten him. Composedly, however, she nodded, thought for a moment of saying something, then kept silent.

'This is the moment I have looked forward to,' he said to her.

Again she nodded — his voice, a long, low, enthusiastic sentence as to his love of the Prelude, ceased for a moment to seem remarkable to her. A slender, slanting spiral of yellow sunlight was shining down on the dark masses of people before her, transfiguring them. Watching it she fancied there were heads like flower-buds, scarlet and cream and blue, others like yellow cheeses or balls. Presently someone pulled a curtain across a window, and there ran a shadow among the heads and her illusion vanished. She sat very still, very pale, waiting. A scent of verbena reached her—mysterious, soft, she could not tell from where. Presently she remembered that for the first time, for many months, her bosom was drenched with it; and it seemed to her suddenly like some delicious anaesthetic, darkening the past, clouding the people, the cherubs, the shadowy windows, banishing Andrew, keeping alive only those senses she needed for music and her joy.

And suddenly she, too, thought: 'It is for this I have waited.'

She held her hands together, her dry lips apart, ready. The pianist returned.

Then, once more, the perfect moment came, was seized, filled with harmony, and passed away in a dark, flowing dream. The single repeated note, more than ever like some heavy raindrop, pale and berry-like, falling in the summer dusk, seemed to drop on her heart. Leaning forward, she felt nervous, despairing and struggling with something. After some moments there came to her the remembrance of Andrew's visit, the thundery weather, the dark room, and of how it seemed to her he had liked it all, the lilac and its scent, the silence, the rain and her playing. In a dazed way she felt glad, recognizing suddenly the beauty and significance of that memory as part of a revelation.

At the end, sitting perfectly still, not applauding, it suddenly seemed to her again that it was for that above all she also had been waiting.

Then Andrew, bending down, inquired in a whisper: 'You enjoyed it?'

'It was wonderful.'

'Yes, wonderful.'

He went on with the same enthusiasm as before. Not knowing what to say to him she remained silent, as if not interested in what he said. And the concert ended.

Outside, however, she felt a sense of guiltiness, experiencing moments when she detested the cool, detached air with which she had listened to him. And now and then, in some deeper moment of reproach for herself, she would talk to him with sudden tenderness, with effusion and delight, knowing that she was impressing him. She laughed often. Her eyes were bright; she looked no longer pale, but flushed and happy, and now and then would hum the air of some nocturne they had heard.

As she leaned from the carriage window to say 'Goodbye,' he suddenly looked anxious and said to her: 'Are you happier?'

It was too sudden. She did not reply and soon afterwards the train moved away. And returning home, staring at the meadows, the farmhouses, the trees and the people at the level-crossings, all looking sleepy in the sunlight, she would constantly repeat those words, telling herself that she did not understand.

IN Andrew Foster's room in Harkloe was a piano which, until he had heard Catherine play, he himself never opened or felt like playing. It stood obscured by books in a corner, the pale, fretted walnut case in places chipped and dusty, some of the gold leaf worn off its German name.

The day after going to the concert with her he felt drawn to it in an extraordinary way, and removing the books, dusted it and opened it. The keys were a faded yellow, the lowest octave produced only a soft, dull tone, and among the upper notes were some which failed to respond.

From his room he could see over the roofs of the town. In the still, sunny air of that evening he could see them spreading out for a great distance, until it seemed that faint white clouds rested on those farthest away. It was warm and he opened his window. A cool spring breeze came in. He began trying to play, at first carelessly, then conscientiously, picking out the air of the Chopin Prelude which had so impressed him the previous day.

An image of Catherine, extraordinarily pale, silent and beautiful, began intruding upon him. He saw her once again in her coat of dark green, her head perfectly erect, her pale, smooth skin giving an effect of something almost exotic against the drab, dirty plaster of the concert-hall. Then he recalled the evening of the thunderstorm. He saw her once again in her thin, graceful dress of some pale, indescribable shade and there returned a memory of the way she had said, 'I

68

shall think of you', in a sad, envious voice, as if she were intensely, insufferably unhappy, longing in her loneliness for something she perhaps had no courage to express and could only go on longing for in that same way.

He rested his hands softly on the faded keys of the piano, and without playing gave himself up to the pleasure of thinking about her. He went through the concert, her late arrival, her conversation and the Prelude. His impressions had been deep and varied. He had noticed unusual things like a thin blue vein beneath one ear, a scratch on a finger and a loop of pink ribbon showing above her mellowing breasts. She had dazzled him a little. Her pallor had set him wondering why she did not sleep at nights, and once again he had become convinced of her unhappiness, her oppression and her longing for something hopelessly and inconceivably beyond her.

'And yet during the Prelude,' he thought, 'she changed and she didn't look at me in that strange way.'

He gave up sitting at the piano, and going to the window where the sunset was visible, radiating its warm green and gold, he stood watching some birds flying over.

He recalled a scent of verbena. How Charles would have detested it! He remembered Catherine saying: 'Five yards of silk, turquoise colour, and there was a row about it.' Over and over again he told himself how perfectly he understood what lay behind it all!

Soon afterwards he went out, and through the close, warm streets walked to the river. A bullfinch was still singing in the willows. Darkness was falling. He pondered once again in a confused, stumbling way on what he felt for her, not knowing if he felt aright. In his own dim intuition he had no faith — it was so clear he might be mistaken about her. And he kept his eyes on the glassy surface of the water and the black, motionless shadows of the rushes and trees by the edge, longing to see everything about her with such perfect faithfulness and beauty.

She was unhappy, he kept thinking. Yet how deeply? What for? Was it his place to alleviate her unhappiness?

He struggled with one question after another. But it seemed to him in the end he knew still no more than that she was beautiful, that she played the piano beautifully and above all that she was unhappy.

When he returned to his room it was dark and stars were shining, scattered like bird-seed. In his room the effect of the piano-keys gleaming white in the corner startled him. The moment he saw them he remembered all unexpectedly her wedding, her sisters, their sweetly low, drowsy voices and the way someone, perhaps she herself, had sung a long plaintive Indian melody he could never perfectly remember.

When he went to bed it was nearly midnight. In spite of everything the time seemed to drag wearily. He was not tired, turned over and over, and could not sleep. Bewildered and troubled he set out to recall the faintest and most distant memories of her. Like a phantom she became immediately elusive. And he felt that if he had been asked at that moment, 'What do you think of her?' he would have replied desperately:

'Not yet. I've not made up my mind about her.'

Constantly he was assailed by the thought of going to see her again. 'I must go,' he would say. 'My God, what a figure! What a look she gave me.' He longed for a repetition of the soft, appealing glances and words she had given him and to know for certain if she were unhappy, and why. 'And yet it's absurd, it will look suspicious,' he would think. At last, as if having stood for an immense space on the brink of a precipice and grown unsteady, he surrendered: 'Perhaps I will go, but not yet, in a week or two, not too soon.'

He found a brief, unsatisfactory refuge in indecision, cursing himself at the same time for the wretched femininity of it all. 'Why worry? Why struggle?' he kept asking himself. Yet something, her tenderness for him, his permanent, realistic and exceedingly lovely memory of her, tortured him into endless and hopeless struggling again.

And then, when he gave in at last, set out on Sunday and walked until afternoon with the expectation of seeing her, she was not at home.

I T was to see the old clerk, Hands, they had gone — in anticipation, in actuality and in retrospect a visit repellent to her. An intense blue sky flooded the square with white sunshine and on the spire pigeons cooed gently, as if nervously, in the quiet air. She had with her a basket of black grapes. Though she displayed nothing she felt nervous also, afraid of the narrow, execrably mean streets through which they had to walk, the smell of a backwater, sour, sluggish and green, running among the houses, and above all of the thought of Hands lying ill in some house similar to those they kept passing and passing.

They spoke very little.

But once, half-afraid, she ventured to ask:

'Is it serious, Hands's illness?'

'It's consumption,' he told her. 'You know that.'

He began next moment going into details, telling her first how one lung was affected, then another, making an oval with his thumb and forefinger and saying: 'Supposing this is the lung. The puncture began there. Then it extended to here. Now there's no hope for him.'

She felt a desire to say to him: 'How do you know? Who told you all this?' but some instinct kept her silent.

Nevertheless she felt intensely repelled by what he had said, at the calm, detached way in which he had spoken, appearing to relish describing things nauseating and terrible to her.

And suddenly at the thought of what it might be like in reality, she shrank back and entreated him:

'Go on without me, I can't come. Take the grapes. I can't come, I can't, I can't!'

She tried to give up the basket, but he refused, took her arm and made her continue.

'Having got so far, you can't go back,' he said. 'Don't be foolish!'

'I can't go! Don't make me,' she implored desperately.

'What's the matter?'

'It's horrible!' she whispered. 'I can't bear it.'

'You must come.'

'I can't! I can't!'

'I give you up,' he said despairingly. 'I don't understand you.'

'But it's the thought of sickness — and perhaps death, I can't bear. Don't you understand that?'

'Yes. I understand that. I understand that. But it's your duty.'

'Ah!'

That blow crushed her into resigning herself bitterly to silence. He appeared to accept it and they went on. The narrow, stifling, unpleasant streets continued until at last Charles paused, passed down a dark entry and knocked on a door at the end. She followed him, not saying a word. In the entry she kicked her foot against a tin in which fish had been kept. In the yard at the end there was a rank smell of cabbage, unclean dogs, a lavatory, stale, bad cooking and filth. Charles knocked twice. At the first knock no one came, but at the second footsteps were heard and a girl of twenty-five or six, thin, hollow-cheeked and epileptic-looking, appeared, half-smiled and motioned them in.

Inside it was cleaner, but she caught the same smell of stale cooking, cabbage and dogs as before. They went down a step into a room — a room to her of depressing dimensions, with a ceiling burnt black in the centre by a lamp, its walls plastered with dark yellow paper covered with shiny patches of grease where bodies had rubbed. She caught sight of an ugly oleograph of Queen Victoria on the wall, another of some soldiers in red. There were a few worn books, a bottle or two and some painted tins on a shelf. In one corner a man of thirty-two or three sat playing with a whippet. Everything seemed to her as if in some once bright-coloured picture, which, having faded, had been daubed over with dirty varnish, and gone on in filthy deterioration still. Depressed, sickened, half-afraid, she waited for the girl to take them through. No one spoke. The whippet turned its sharp head and looked at her with bright eyes. She felt as if she had intruded and was unwanted, and longed in that moment, as never before, to be back in the still, sultry streets again, under the blue sky.

'Come up,' said the girl.

They followed her. Upstairs it seemed cleaner, there was more light and on the landing, at least, there was no smell. Yet she remained depressed and would, she felt, have retreated at the slightest sign.

On the landing she whispered to Charles:

'Who are these people?'

'Hands's children — a nuisance, all of them. They've dragged him down,' he answered.

She was silent, thinking, 'How terrible! What misery!' and was seized at the moment with a feeling of profound pity, torturing, reproachful and vain, trying, hopelessly, to conceive of something she could say or do to alleviate that distress.

At that moment a door opened, the girl said: 'It's Mr. Foster,' and they entered the bedroom.

74

There it was cleanest of all. The bed and the walls were dead white. The sun made in one corner a perfect triangle of gold, a dark cobweb at the apex, one angle touching the iron bed where Hands lay. She saw it first, and thinking 'Perhaps, after all, it's not so terrible,' stood waiting. A little woman with a slop-pail in her hands set it down and came to her and in a voice obviously changed by her coming, said: 'He's been asking about you.'

She gave her the grapes. The woman took the basket, made an expression of deep thankfulness, rubbed her hands across the dark bloom of the grapes, that bloom she had thought so luxuriant and perfect, and set them aside.

Suddenly she saw Hands for the first time since that day she had grown angry with him. She stood still, amazed, shocked, staring at him. And for a moment or two it seemed to her that she was not gazing at Hands himself, but at a ghost of him, terrifying in its emaciation, its yellowness, its air of decay. She saw him look at her, fail to recognize her, look again. And the second time his stare remained, transfixing her, frightening her. 'He can't see me,' she thought desperately. But she remained unconsoled, aware suddenly that the pale, washed-out gaze had life, even though life so remote and faint as to be like that of a sun behind an opaque winter cloud, without warmth, without any other power than was needed merely to distinguish twilight from darkness or existence from death. She saw that not only the eyes, but the skin, the hair, the lips, the fingers and the whole expression of Hands were becoming overpowered by decay. And she felt no longer a sense of pity, but of something amounting almost to a shameful terror.

75

At her side, at the moment which seemed worst to her, Charles said:

'How are you today?'

To her it seemed the only answer could have been, 'A little nearer death', but no answer came, only a long, pitiful look which sought to convey something definite, but faded, having conveyed only a sense of approaching nothingness.

She felt sick. Then, as if such a look had not been enough, she caught suddenly a mixture of smells, different, more delicate and yet more nauseating even than those below. An odd, faint odour of sweat reached her, a smell of drugs and milk, then the stench from the slop-pail, lastly that intangible, horrible smell that clings with disease and the suspicion of death. Looking down she saw under the bed a vessel stained with blood and phlegm.

She could not help that glance, and, as it happened, Hands caught it as he lay staring. She saw his eyes fill at once with tears, watched them run helplessly over his cheeks, and recognized why he wept, understanding the poor, pitiful grief of his helplessness, his ability to perform not even a primitive function alone. The long, silent flow of tears, the voice of Mrs. Hands saying, 'Give over now — it'll never do, you'll be worse again!' moved her to deeper pity, more searching agony. Yet she did nothing. And Hands continued like a child in his fretting and crying.

She wanted to say to Charles. 'Take me away — let's go,' but nothing came.

In despair she gazed at the objects in the room, the brass bed-knobs, a picture, the grapes, the wall-paper, then at the sunshine, the roofs and the sky beyond the windows. Lastly she was drawn to watch Hands's wife, and suddenly the tenderness, capability and knowledge of that woman as she moved certainly, pityingly about the bed, comforting her grey, wasted wreck as if he had been fresh, lovely and like a child, with life before him, seemed to her stupendously wonderful.

Unable suddenly to bear this mixture of hardship and suffering and pity, she crossed to the window and gazed out, breathing heavily.

She saw nothing to help her or renew her fortitude. Behind her Hands began coughing, a low, rattling cough which she understood would end in exhaustion. Listening to it was like listening to some engine which, once started, will go on until its fuel is consumed. That terrible evidence of pain and suffering, the most terrible she had ever known, tortured her.

As she stood there, not daring to look at the shaking figure behind, she thought, 'It will never end, he will never survive it.' Trembling, afraid, she searched herself for fortitude and finding none excused herself. 'It's so awful, it's so terrible.' But the coughing did not cease. The thought of Hands dying did not cease. She shut her eyes, clasping her hands.

A voice behind her asked, 'Shall we go?'

For a moment she could not reply. Then she whispered only:

'It would be best.'

They crossed the room with all its terrible features assailing her again, the stench of drugs and the slop-pail, the smell of sickness and death. She saw Hands lying on his side, a pan against his chest, his head lolling feebly, his only protestation against his affliction. The pan was full of blood, the bedsheets were stained a greenish scarlet. She felt in that moment that she had never known, seen, or dreamed that such wretchedness could exist. Most of all she prayed never to see it again.

'Please let's go,' she begged.

They went. Along the landing, on the stairs and in the room below Hands's coughing was audible — and then even in the yard, the entry and the street outside, so that she noticed the unpleasant smell and the sultriness no more.

'Why should it be so?' she kept asking herself. 'God — why should it?'

They walked on in silence. Charles took her hand. She was fretful and felt like weeping. But gradually what had passed took on the significance of a dream, still terrible, still agonizing, but no longer a reality. The touch of Charles's hand on hers seemed to her something more sweet, more soothing and tender than she had ever known. She laid her head against his shoulder.

'Walk slowly,' she said.

They did so. They kept silent, as if afraid of speaking. And for the rest of that day it seemed to her that her own life with its dull monotony, its misunderstandings and petty cares had become tolerable at last.

CHAPTER FIVE

THREE mornings later Hands died. It happened that Charles was present. The end had been terrible. At dinner she could eat nothing and listened to what Charles said with a sort of numb horror, grasping everything slowly, by painful degrees. He told her the details in a heavy, laboured way, describing the sufferings, the struggle, the rattle in the throat, the ghastly cough 'that threw the blood over the sheets,' the groaning, the despair.

At last she could endure it no longer and got up, half-shouting:

'Be quiet! I can't stand it. I know enough already.'

'What are you saying?'

'I can't stand it! I've seen it all! It's terrible — I feel sick with it.'

She opened a window, stood looking out, breathing hard.

'What's come over you lately?' Charles said.

'What's that?' she asked.

'What is it? What's come over you?'

She paused. 'If I tell you — shall you understand?' she said.

'Of course.'

'Well,' — she faltered — 'no, after all I won't tell you. You won't understand.'

'Come, what is it? Are you ill?'

'I won't tell you! Go away! I don't want to tell you!'

'Listen to me. Sit down.'

She remained standing. Silence came. She felt sick, confused, angry, able to gather neither her thoughts nor the strength even to tell him: 'I am unhappy. You are making my life wretched. We are a burden to each other,' as she felt she must do. Once or twice she struggled to tell him, constructing the first sentence in different ways in her mind and then desisting, telling herself that sooner or later, by her increasingly distant manner, her coldness and indifference, he would understand it all.

She stood motionless. In the garden a chaffinch was chirruping in the branches of an apple tree. She listened to it, watched it move from branch to branch, never still, and suddenly it seemed to her that though it was summer and everywhere heavy, luxuriant and lovely, she was somehow missing it, not seeing or feeling it as she had done before. She was bound up with something drab and repellent to her, with Charles, with the everlasting smell of corn and clover, the same street, and now with Hands and with death. She seemed only half alive. She knew it and felt it. Yet she could never change it. With a sort of inquiring pity she would look at the sky, the trees, the sleepy jasmine on the arch and the young fruit on the wall, as if seeking encouragement. And then she would ask herself — 'Encouragement for what? What do I want? Where should I go if I was courageous? What should I do?'

It struck her suddenly that she was certain only as to the things she could not do — that she could not endure pettiness, meanness or cavilling, above all that she could not think or talk of death.

Suddenly Charles got up, came to her and said:

'They have been good enough to ask us to go to the funeral. You will come, of course?'

'God! Don't talk of it!'

'What do you mean? Surely you understand?' he

asked in a calm voice. 'What will they say? He was employed here for nearly fifty years.'

'It's horrible! Why should I go?'

'It shows respect. They will like it.'

'Like it!'

'Appreciate it. You are my wife, aren't you?'

Not knowing what to say she walked away from him, he following her, arguing, beseeching.

'Don't follow me!' she suddenly cried. 'I'm not the hearse! For God's sake!' She felt goaded, reckless, her colour rising as she looked at him, her heart beating heavily.

'What terrible things you say!' he reproached her.

'Oh! what matter?'

She sank into a chair, covering her face with her hands, shutting out the blue sky, the tree-tops and the sunlight simply in order to shut out him too, and began repeating in a low voice, insistently, nothing else but the words:

'Go away, go away.'

She heard him go at last. After that by silence, by things she said, by her looks and above all her detached aloof air, she continued trying to make him understand that she would not go.

But he constantly returned to the subject and would follow her about, entreating her:

'Catherine, think a moment. Think what it means.'

She would remain adamant, keeping silent for fear of another unpleasant scene. And then perhaps he would insist:

'Listen to me. Let me explain. He was employed here for — '

'Don't!' she would entreat. 'I can't bear it.'

'Why can't you?'

'It's detestable to me, the wretchedness and everything. Don't ask me! It's unbearable. All your conventions are unbearable.'

Charles stood still, looking at her in a stupid, injured way, as if not quite understanding, his eyes showing wide margins of white. Suddenly, unable to bear this, she burst out:

'Don't stare! Oh! Why did you marry me?'

He bore this for a moment without speaking, as if overwhelmed. Then in a low voice he entreated:

'Catherine, Catherine!'

'Oh! for God's sake!'

She turned to go, but in doing so she faced him, and saw suddenly in his eyes an expression she had never seen there, dull, apathetic, bewildered, as if he still did not grasp what she had said. And for a moment she felt sorry for him, despising herself, ready to make amends, half afraid of the way they were drifting apart. And she put up her hands immediately, touched him, and said:

'Did it sound terrible? I'm sorry. Forgive me. Try and forget all that.'

He was silent after she had touched him, and he looked at her imploringly for a moment, then said:

'You didn't mean it? It's a mistake? You will come to the funeral? You understand?'

For a moment she stared, then abruptly she came to herself, pained and horrified at his lack of insight, intelligence, understanding, pity — all the virtues which would have prevented the words 'You will come to the funeral?' And it seemed to her he was not merely stupid, but selfish and callous, and feeling that she could no longer bear it, she ran up to her bedroom, where she flung herself across the bed, angry, dissatisfied, mistrustful, hating him, hating Hands for dying, detesting, shrinking from her life and herself again.

All that began once more a longing for escape, for something beautiful and different in life. Unable to find it, and seeing Charles as the cause of it all, she began to treat him with contempt, with indifference, with prolonged sulkiness and obstinacy. At night she put her face into the pillow and repeated to herself, 'God, this miserable going on! Why is it?' She tried to take up reading, failed, and for consolation would go out, and lying on that part of the lawn where the fragrance of the currant-bushes and pinks hung strong and intoxicating, would watch the rooks fly over, idly turn the pages of some book, and dream. When she tried to play the piano she was not successful; something seemed lacking. She began to experience fits of depression. Worst of all she would catch herself saying again and again when about to do something:

'No, no. It's not worth while.'

THE thought sometimes occurred to her that lately Andrew had not been to see them, and in a half-languid, half-perplexed way she wondered about him. Recalling his visits, and above all the concert, she remembered that she had been happy and she found herself unconsciously looking forward to his coming again. Sometimes she remembered how he had gazed at her and said: 'Are you happier now?' and she had not understood him.

On the day of Hands's funeral, when it was sultry and Charles had looked uncomfortable and perspiring in his black clothes, and the leaves drooped in a day which had no more life than a collapsed balloon, he came again. Over the edges of the roofs the heat shimmered and danced. In the garden the heads of the sunflowers and marigolds, lolling heavily, swung against her skirt and back into stillness as she passed.

On arriving he looked tired, his cheeks pale and thin. She fetched out her shawl, however, and on the red patch it made in the grass under the trees he sat down by her and recovered.

They did not speak much. Then desultorily they began discussing music, and he began telling her that in London, on business, he had heard some young violinist whose playing had seemed to him so utterly different, so stupendous and wonderful, that he felt he must come and relate it all. He twined some grass round his fingers as he spoke. Gradually, like the grass curling in a green spiral over his hands, the things he said, his quiet, earnest way of speaking, and the pleasure in his voice, began to affect her, insinuating themselves into her existence like some fresh growth, a green shoot in some rank, neglected darkness. She felt happy, sitting with her hands pressed into cheeks, looking at the church, which, rising abruptly out of a mass of roofs, elms and sycamore trees, looked taller and more graceful than she had ever known. And sitting here, the summer stillness making his voice drowsy, she imagined herself climbing it, step by step, until she could look down with a sort of contempt on the house, the carts in the yard, the limes, the chemist's and everything distasteful to her. And intoxicated, venturesome yet certain, missing nothing, in imagination she climbed it again and again.

As he talked on, quiet, hesitating, almost nonchalant, suddenly it came to her that here, perhaps, was what she needed, had longed for, had felt she must have. She had no name for it. It was intangible, not easy to grasp. Experiencing it, however, she felt refreshed, her anxiety and despondency vanished.

Suddenly it was so pleasant to her that she rose and leaned against an apple tree. She shook the trunk gently, so that the leaves sighed. He noticed this, and asked why it was. She would only reply:

'I'm happy, that's all! I'm happy!'

She remembered the day she had flung crumbs on the water at the picnic and had repeated also: 'I'm happy, that's all! I'm happy!' Now, gazing down at him as he lay on the red shawl, she felt that he understood how rare, precious and lovely such moments were to her. From that moment, because of that understanding, she felt things differently. The sky, brighter and more lovely, seemed to resemble something — a silk cushion, she thought, a blue hat — something ridiculous, in all conscience, but what matter?

The grass, the sunflowers, the fruit trees all seemed different. In a leaf she suddenly plucked off a currant bush she became aware of thousands of veins, wrinkles and crosses, things she had missed all her life before, but which seemed, now, to make that leaf a strange, marvellous and significant thing. And she kept it in her hand, wondering and remarking on its beauty.

He sat watching. Presently she became aware of this watching and felt, as during the thunderstorm and at the concert, uneasy, hardly knowing what to do. She simply stood still, a little distance off, and then, gazing at the leaf, asked:

'If I make tea, will you have lemon with it?'

'Please don't trouble.'

But she disregarded him, went away and returned soon afterwards with a tray. She poured out tea. He halved a lemon. She watched him slip his slice gently into his cup, steer it round and round, submerge it, let it rise to the surface again, 'Like a boat,' he said, not looking up. And she was reminded of the river, the picnic under the willow trees, the meadows, the haymaking and the man who had gone downstream singing.

And she felt she must ask: 'Do you spend any time on the river?'

'Yes, I'm fond of it,' he said.

'In the old days,' she began, looking suddenly dreamy, 'we used to spend four or five nights on the river every week in summer. It was jolly. We were such idiots. We made everything as absurd as we could. We couldn't row, but somehow we used to get along, shouting and laughing, nearly upsetting other people, and probably being a great nuisance, and yet enjoying it all enormously.'

86

'Yes. Charles used to come home disapproving it all.'

She cried without hesitation, 'Oh, really! And yet I quite believe it!'

She laughed and he joined in. She felt intensely happy. The present and the recollection of the past seemed for one moment to unite and harmonize perfectly. She kept on laughing.

'You know it's the regatta next week?' he asked her suddenly.

'The regatta? Where? What day?'

'At Harkloe, on Saturday.'

And then, just as at the concert and the picnic, nothing would satisfy her but endless discussion about that regatta, what happened there, the colours, the dresses, the races, the crowds, the excitement, the glamour, the chains of tiny lanterns lit in the evening. She besieged him with questions, flushing in her enthusiasm, not content unless every detail was explained, enlarged upon. She became aware, little by little, without ever having dreamed of it, of enthusiasm rising in him also, imparting a strange, more than ever hesitant touch to what he said, a sort of restless eagerness even to the way he went on playing with the lemon in his tea while gazing at her with nervous, unsteady and admiring eyes.

They talked in that way until Charles returned. She ran straight to him. Oddly enough, the black suit, the ugly hard hat and his seriousness did not affect her. She only said to him, repeating it:

'Let's go to the regatta! Let's go to the regatta!'

She explained everything. Once again she felt sorry for him with his dull, apathetic smile, his worn-out air, his sad look of surprise, and it occurred to her: 'Perhaps

the funeral has made him ill-tempered and depressed,'
and going up to him she put her arm in his, squeezed it
and said:

'Let's go! It's so exciting. Let's go. You'd like it too!'

He paused, then said simply: 'I could do with a bit of
excitement myself,' at which, understanding it to mean
'Yes', she flung out her arms in a spasm of naive,
exaggerated delight.

IT was the second day of July, a date which had become impressed on her mind unforgettably, as if by a seal.

In the train, happy again, amused easily, she talked a great deal. Only at odd moments, without warning, she would become intensely silent, as if preparing for something. Once she fell into conversation with a little stout man who persisted in telling her: 'There's never a day passes but what me and my old woman have a cross word, but we're happy!'

She laughed at him, and at times laughed also at Charles, sitting with an umbrella between his knees, then at herself, her reflection in the window, at the thought of the regatta; and then at nothing. Always she was conscious of being a little removed from the rest of humanity as she saw it in the railway carriage, Charles, the stout man, his wife, the children, and the country-women going to market. In her own strange, elevated way she would catch herself pitying their dull thoughts, their drab lives. All the time her hands were nervously tying and untying the silk bow at her breast.

The air was sultry and sometimes Charles nodded, but to her the warm drowsiness seemed refreshing, and whenever he gazed into the sky and informed her: 'There will be rain, you'll see,' she only shook her sunshade and laughed at him.

At the station Andrew met them. He had brought a friend, a young journalist who was going to write a description of the events and had a special hired boat from which they would be able to watch the races.

They came to the river. She was suddenly astonished to see crowds of people on both banks, the stream itself full of boats, the trees festooned, long lines of little triangular flags drooping between the branches. The pale, bluish water was ruffled and eddied, full of reflections and lights of all colours, red swimming with black, green and gold. From the boats Japanese sunshades lolled and drooped. Everywhere people were laughing, talking, calling greetings and remarks to each other. Now and then someone would shout through a megaphone, like a giant disturbed, and in the brief hush a gramophone would go on playing its tune as if mocking. At one spot a band was getting ready to play, the instruments flashing brassily in the sun, the men pom-pom-ming and trilling before beginning. And through the trees, behind it all, still and silent in the sunshine, she now and then caught glimpses of meadows stretching far away in a picture of cool, tranquil green.

After some delay, during which she chattered much and was alternately annoyed and amused at Charles's persistent 'I hope it'll keep fine. I hope so!' they rowed off.

She sat at the rudder. Andrew and the journalist were to take the rowing in turns; now the journalist was rowing. Cool, yet nervously delighted with the colours, the noise and the excitement, she sat upright, watching the other boats, the people in them and on the bank, and then their long distorted shadows swaying like thick black and coloured reeds in the water. Now the river seemed more crowded than ever. Yet sometimes she caught strange, unexpected glimpses of a soft intense blue mirrored among the confusion without a ruffle or shadow. They rowed slowly, taking long pauses. During one of these intervals, she found herself suddenly struck by the incongruity of the three men in the boat with her; at her side Charles, wearing his thick tweed, looking commonplace and sometimes faintly supercilious, as if disapproving it all; then the journalist with his soft, pleasant manner, smiling at her as he rested on the oars; then lastly Andrew gazing at everything with a way she felt was peculiar to him — intense, faintly frowning, as if resenting or questioning something. And once, during a longer pause than usual, she longed to lean forward and ask him what that something was; if it were the patches of reflected sky, the people, the noise, or the sunlight dancing on the water. But she did nothing and kept still, thinking for the first time, without any attempt at concealment, how glad she was to have him in the boat with her.

There were periods when she did nothing but chatter light-heartedly and in which she caught herself saying things she did not mean, foolish things which made Charles and the journalist laugh. Sometimes she would be struck by the shallowness and emptiness of their laughter.

They rowed at last to the spot from which they were to see the races. There, under a great willow tree which hung down and touched the water, it was cooler, and Catherine lay back in the boat, staring at the blue sky through the leaves, relaxing tranquilly. Charles, Andrew and the journalist lit cigarettes and sat talking.

Suddenly she found herself once again becoming engrossed in the contemplation of their faces, thinking how incongruous they were, detaching herself from them and regarding them in her cool, elevated way. Once more the expression of Andrew's face arrested her, troubling her by its absorption, its restlessness, its intensity; and again the longing would seize her to know what he brooded upon and if it were making him unhappy. But again she said nothing; again she sat only staring, wondering, her suspicions awaking and retreating, her heart filled with a sort of brooding, too. It was a relief when the races began. But though she liked the sight of the white crews darting down the stream in the sunshine, the shouts, the excitement and the cheering, it was not as she had expected it to be. She felt at times uneasy, distracted by something. In order to get rid of the feeling she stood up in the boat and, in spite of warnings by Charles, shouted and clapped her hands.

'Don't get excited, you'll upset the boat!' he would say to her.

'It doesn't matter! I can't help it!' she would reply.

Nevertheless she would sit down again. Now, sometimes, the colours, the noise and the continual sight of the boats, as if one race were being rowed over and over again, irritated her. Then she was worried more and more by Andrew, who appeared to have lost interest in everything, but only now and then gave her strange, purposeful looks, as if he wished to ask her something.

She lost some of her gaiety. She fell to staring at the journalist, making pencil notes on his programme, and from the journalist to Charles, drowsy even as he watched the races; and then, last of all, at Andrew again, until it seemed he must have become conscious of that watching.

At last she could not bear it, and declared: 'I'm tired of all this racing up and down; let's go ashore and do something else.'

'Who says some tea, in that case?' said Charles.

In one of the intervals they rowed back. Now

92

Andrew was rowing; and lying back against the rudder, impatient of the long stoppages and the noisy crowds on either side, she would find herself watching the slow movement of his young, wiry body, of the oars breasting the water and the stream moving slowly by. Once she gazed upward, and in that moment felt as if drifting somewhere, drifting in the slow, dreamy way that enchanted her, until she felt lost, entranced by some strange, pleasant wonder, sad no more.

When they came ashore she felt dazed and hardly heard Charles saying: 'Well, the clouds are coming, my friends. There'll be rain yet, you'll see.' And for a few moments longer she moved in this dream in which, of concrete things, only the meadows, the sunshine, the river and Andrew had any longer a part.

Then Charles said: 'The marquee for tea — what do you say?' and she found herself walking side by side with the three men towards it. At the sight of that immense marquee, crowded with people, its vast interior full of a greenish gloomy light, she shrank into herself. On the threshold Charles saw a table, ran to it, put his umbrella across it and cried, 'Here we are, in luck again,' and they followed him. Since leaving the boat she had scarcely spoken, and now, imprisoned under the green flabby roof of the marquee, an increasing din of voices, crockery and eating going on about her, she felt utterly dumb, longing once more for the river and the sunshine, wondering why she had ever let them slip away.

Suddenly Charles rose and shouted to someone: 'This way, friends; come and sit with us!' She saw, of all people, the Galloways coming across. A sense of awful irritation seized her. She spoke in a distant voice and, when they had been waited upon, poured out tea for the six people as if she were pouring out, without the faintest hope of ever regaining it again, all the happiness she had ever known.

Charles, the Galloways and the journalist began discussing the races. The Galloways had shut up their shop for the afternoon. The woman reiterated: 'It's an event for us, you know, and we think it's so lovely, the weather, the boaters and everything. And I'm sure we're thankful.' The journalist began reading the names of those who had won the races. Everyone talked at once. Charles ate jam tarts in one bite and caused amusement by mimicking someone finishing a race. He perspired, his hair hanging down, his expression fierce and ridiculous enough for her to long to get up and shout at him: 'For God's sake stop! I can't stand it any more!'

But she kept silent. All the things she detested seemed to be repeated purposely, over and over again. Only now and then she would notice that Andrew never spoke or took part in it all.

They trooped out of the marquee at last. Charles, the journalist and the Galloways were for watching the races again. She had not the heart to protest. The crowd was thicker than ever, the air sultrier, and the river had a dull, troubled look when the sun went in. The chatter of voices had a sharp, insistent sound. Now and then she would ask herself:

'How much longer will it go on? When will it end?'

Suddenly someone said: 'Mark my words, it'll rain before long.'

'Well, I told you!' Charles's voice rang out. 'I prophesied it.'

Again she felt furious with him, hating passionately his cocksureness, his amiability, his absurd umbrella,

as she hated the noise, the trivial talk and the excitement about the races.

Rain, beginning at first in isolated drops which fell
on the river like flies, then more threateningly, fell at
last thickly, beating on the river like hail. Everyone
ran for the trees and the marquee. The Galloways and
the journalist ran back to the marquee, while Charles,
Andrew and herself sheltered under the umbrella,
watching two drenched crews finishing a race in the
shower. The river looked purple, splashed with rings of
silver, its banks a strange, lurid green under the surly
clouds.

'No more than I expected,' Charles kept repeating.
'I said it all the time.'

That preposterous repetition infuriated her. Not
speaking, she longed for something to change it all.
She bit her lips as she stared out at the raining sky.

'Only a summer shower,' she heard someone remark.

It struck her then that without Charles and the noisy,
sheltering crowds, that shower would have been
beautiful, memorable, an event she would have long
afterwards looked wistfully back upon and cherished.

And when, soon after, the rain slackened and
Charles left them, saying: 'I'll run over to the marquee
to see what the rest are doing,' she remained there in
silence, watchful as ever of the rain dripping off the
willow leaves, the clouds looming across, people darting
out of sheltered spots and magically disappearing again,
of the river with its clusters of empty boats moored
under the trees, and of Andrew, at whom she would
sometimes covertly glance, smile, and then, as if afraid
of something, look away again without a word.

A CIRCUS came to the town that week. Early one morning she saw it arrive, a very long train of caravans, with wagons drawn by steam-engines, and groups of four or five creamy, piebald horses, all heralded by a man on horseback, with a scarlet hunter's coat and a copper trumpet on which he blew ringing blasts to attract attention.

It crossed the square like a medieval pageant, looking most gay in the sunshine. She was at a bedroom window, watching it, when Charles ran out. He had on a white smock, such as barbers wear, and seemed very excited at so many horses.

She heard him say to his foreman, who wore a grey smock:

'A lot of horses like that don't live on air. They'll take some pounds' worth of fodder, eh?'

'Better tackle them when the tents are up, sir.'

'I'll go up in an hour or two. A nice picture, aren't they? What is the finest cut we can make on the price of straw?'

They disappeared, presumably to work out a list of very keen prices, a matter on which Charles was very astute.

She left the window, crossed the room and entered a smaller bedroom. Before the blast of the trumpet had aroused her she had been sitting on the bed. It was a sweet, pale, sunny room, with a pretty blue water-jug and delicate embroidery on the pillow-slips. Visitors always had this room. She had been sitting in a reverie thinking of the likelihood of Andrew staying overnight, when he came again, and it had been strangely thrilling to think of him sleeping there.

During the week all kinds of bright, sad and alluring thoughts had tormented her. The scene by the river, in the storm, often recurred, its many meanings flashing on her like lights from a precious stone.

It was now Saturday, the day on which he would have a half-holiday, and when she expected he would come. She was happy in a totally new, dancing kind of way as she sat smoothing the bed-linen with her fingers. The expectation of looking forward to some bright event gave her face a lovely, excited look. The sunshine, the summer, and the air laden with heavy odours made life seem rich and fragrant with happy possibilities.

But the morning passed slowly until eleven, when Charles came in for a cup of coffee before going to the circus.

'Would you like to come?' he asked cheerfully.

She was at first silent, then presently said she would come.

The circus was being pitched in a field behind the church. There was much confusion and noise as they arrived. Cream, roan, milk-white and dark reddish piebald ponies were being led towards low tents to be stabled or were tied to posts in a corner of the field. A tent with a white dome had been erected and a heap of flags of various nations, ready to be hoisted, lay strewn on the steps of a smart white van. A small army of men, quite ordinary-looking except for a crimson or blue-checked shirt here and there, were busy with stakes, rigging and animals. Two small mangy elephants had been tethered apart from the tents and vans. Looking rather afraid, a baker's boy hurried through with a basket of warm loaves. From a van-window a woman shouted a rude remark to someone invisible, and a man was swearing vociferously inside one of the tents. There was a thick, predominating smell of animal dung, and everything had something of the drab, devitalized look that a theatre has during early morning.

They were directed to the manager's tent by a local butcher, who had been doing business too.

'Will you stay outside or will you come in?' Charles asked her. 'I shan't be long. These fellows haven't much time to wait.'

She went in.

The manager was a big, assertive and obviously keen customer with a brown moustache. Catherine sat down on a sugar-box while Charles did business with him.

She did not trouble to follow their conversation. During every moment of silence now it became sweet and essential for her to devote herself to the thought of Andrew. This time her thoughts assumed a quiet tone, with a faint, vague ache behind.

As she sat there in this unassuming pose one of the circus hands came in. He saw the manager engaged, but instead of withdrawing, lolled against a post and watched her.

It was an unequivocal, daring, appraising stare. Obviously he thought her quite beautiful. He gave no smile. Instead his eyes were level, soft and pensive in their expression, and his lips drooping. She wondered why anyone should look at her like that, and a certain uneasiness seized her, inexplicable until it flashed upon her that the essentials of the expression were those she had so often seen in Andrew.

After that she had no peace. It did not matter to her that Charles had received an order for fodder at a good price and some free tickets for the evening performance. She left the circus-ground without a repetition of the impressions she had received on coming in.

All this was a sweet turmoil to have been thus begun, to be lived over and over again and to prolong. To lie in the small bedroom and press her cheek against the pillow simply because his cheek might one day be pressed there was a subtle association with him; each clanging of the bell in the kitchen that was a disappointment was also part of an exciting ache; and while picking some pinks and marigolds beyond the house she sank down, pressed her hands deep in her bosom and thought of him for the first time as a lover.

Then, towards evening, he came.

Charles was upstairs, dressing. They sat down where they had first sat together. Now the room was quite bright; only the shadows of plum-leaves danced on the floor.

'Your cheeks are quite red,' he told her suddenly. He knew it was unusual in her.

'I've been running about,' she told him. 'You see, we're going to the circus.'

'A circus?'

'Yes. You'll come, of course. And then stay the night with us?'

He said he would.

'Let's go into the garden then,' she said.

They entered cool shadowy paths worming under the trees. The wilderness of flowers that had been promised in the spring had now come; splashes of blue and white and yellow and scarlet lay in bowers and tiny forests of green. She felt she could not speak. The scent of some evening primroses and mignonette made her catch her breath. The brushing of the stalks and flowers against her fingers startled her. To all this was added the strange sense that the world of practical life had ended and that this screen of coloured loveliness was about to part and admit her into some hushed sweet paradise.

'You were expecting me?' he then said suddenly.

Words seemed too short and bare to answer this. She only nodded her head long and slow.

'You knew I would come,' he said.

Her nodding did not cease.

Her senses seemed rich, vibrant things. Even so late as this a thrush began singing in a cherry tree. It seemed like the sweet overture to a play. While she was watching and listening to it Andrew, attracted by an orange rose, plucked it and brought it for her.

'Pin it in your bosom,' he said to her.

With shining eyes she bent and found a pin in her skirt. She hung the orange rose head downwards at the shallowest point of her breast.

'No, let it hold up its head,' he urged.

So she arranged it to look like a cool orange bud growing up from her white flesh. In doing so she pricked one finger. When she showed it him a spot of blood as large as a dewdrop hung ready to fall.

He dried the blood. To be touched by him was an exquisite, intense happening. The meaning of a certain kind of deep, rapturous absorbed glance between two people, once unfathomed, now became clear as she looked at him. Nothing was said, and silence, their own silence, the silence of leaves and birds, made it seem as if they were for one moment sealed in a quiet casket, the beauty of which had never been surpassed for her.

Then Charles called her name from the door:

'Catherine! Catherine!'

Her mother and sisters had always called her Cathy. She saw a look of annoyance pass over Andrew's face. But he followed her into the house.

'Do you know what time it is?' Charles asked when she entered.

She was too flushed to speak and ran quickly upstairs.

'Don't be all day!' he called after her.

She did not heed, but was all in haste to rearrange her hair. In colour it was like some late blackberry, having a rich lustrous bloom; it spread out straight and thickly woven and never curled. Now she sat down, brushed it swiftly, and fashioned it levelly like the wings of a dark bird, in a most striking way.

Through her head, as she sat before the mirror, kept racing the words: 'You knew I would come,' and to gaze at the reflection of the orange rose made her delight wild.

Only Andrew noticed the mode of her hair and he conveyed his pleasure in quick, repeated looks at her.

Those looks were continued as they sat in the circus. She sat between the two brothers. The circus had changed; bright lights were suspended in the roof and rows of seats had been erected. The air was all animation. The ring received the brightest light. At one end a band was tuning up its instruments, making ridiculous noises from its little scarlet stand, built with just the faintest resemblance to a pavilion at a tournament for a king.

She chatted gaily, with moments of silent misgiving at the strained attitude of the brothers. The absolute realization of her position was still to strike her. Now she was exultantly happy since one had noticed and touched her and because of her pricked finger and the rose.

Some galloping ponies were the first item. She adored the ponies and sat erect and watchful. Then came a whisper:

'Does your finger hurt you now?'

He had touched her.

From that moment she was never at rest. Ponies, chalked clowns, acrobats, jugglers, trick-cyclists and elephants lost their fascination, even so that sometimes she could not look at them. She ceased talking. What filled her now was a longing to be outside talking with Andrew while he pressed her hand, in the garden, where a heavy, odoured darkness would have fallen; and prompted by this she sometimes put out her hand and touched him too.

The pom-pomming of the band never ceased. Charles applauded each item by banging his hands very heavily on his knees, his eyes shining like a boy's.

Suddenly she whispered to the other in a flash:

'The tickets were free, you know.'

It was said impishly, as she might have thrown a dart. He laughed alluringly, in full appreciation, and it sealed their sympathy, as it seemed, for ever after.

Her whole being seemed alive and expectant as they walked home when it was all over. The sky was dull blue and starred and a sultriness ladened the wind. Andrew's face under a lamp was to her the expression of a soul uplifted and enchanted, like her own, and as she looked at it she did not know whether to laugh, keep silent or weep.

Her silence was full of crying thoughts. The house seemed hot and unbearable. Affected by the warm night, Charles took off his boots and sprawled in a chair. She dared not look at him.

'Play the piano,' Charles asked after a moment or two.

She looked urgently at Andrew. He gave no sign.

After consideration she began playing. At first even a more simple Chopin nocturne seemed desultory. She had read of people expressing a mood by music, but her own was diffident in its profound, precious quality and it seemed to her she played badly. She took her hands away from the keys at last with thankfulness.

'Play something with a tune in it — not that stuff.' It was Charles's old objection. 'Play that thing the circus band played.'

'I don't remember.'

'Oh! you know!'

He gave in a bass hum his version of it.

She gazed despairingly at Andrew.

One attempt, not very determined and in the wrong key, set Charles jogging and bumping one stockinged foot. 'Go on! Go on!' he urged. 'You've almost got it!'

But suddenly she drifted, as it were unconsciously, into a prelude, and in this she half-expressed her mood. Andrew did not miss the fine, sensuous excitement in her playing, the sudden, familiar journeys of her fingers, the sheer, physical beauty of her breasts and arms. Bodily and spiritually she seemed very beautiful to him.

He felt he understood to perfection the difficulty of her position. At the end he clapped gently and said:

'Bravo, bravo!'

Charles showed his resentment at once. All music that possessed no tune was not music, he said. Why didn't she go on playing the circus things?

'The circus thing is fifth-rate and horrible,' broke in Andrew, 'otherwise it wouldn't be played in a circus.'

'Prove it, prove it.'

'Your own sense tells you that.'

'My own sense tells me what I like and what I don't like!' Charles banged a book.

'That's different.'

The quietness of his brother's voice aroused Charles. 'Anyway,' he burst forth angrily, 'you'll agree it's better to know what you like and like it than — '

'Of course. Isn't that a platitude?'

Charles grew intensely dogmatic; his eyes were full of resentment.

'Well, I like what I like,' he declared, 'platitude or no platitude.'

'But that's another.'

Charles looked indignant almost to fierceness. She did not understand all that lay behind this antagonistic attitude of the brothers. It was plain that Charles felt disgust and a sort of pompous dislike for Andrew, while Andrew had for Charles a cool, unspeakable contempt.

By some kind of intuition, as if looking into the future, she deplored all this, wished to avoid it, felt that it was full of danger.

And she appeared suddenly gay and indifferent. A few impromptu steps of a dance, during which she scolded them both like children, made them silent again.

'Don't badger — arguing is quite useless — you *are* silly creatures!' she called them.

'But it's always this stuff without a tune in it,' Charles began again. 'Mournful as a sick cat it sounds to me.'

'What will you have then? A dance, a one-step, a waltz?' she bantered.

She feigned seriousness. Intuition told her again how important it was to avoid a quarrel between the two men. Some even finer sense of subtlety told her she herself must not anger Charles. She went and stroked his hair and said:

'You're in such a bad humour. What would you like? *Lieder ohne Wort?*'

'Do I know it?'

'You know this one.'

She played that one she knew he understood and liked most, feeling more at ease now. It effected that compromise she knew he sometimes strove for — to be able to congratulate himself inwardly, 'I am listening to classical music,' and yet enjoy a tune.

'That's all right,' he said at the end. 'Nice tune.'

'Shall I play another?' She sounded dutiful and sweet.

'Just one more — and then supper,' he asked.

She played, and his unsuspecting senses responded in the right way.

In order to complete the effect she waited on him first during supper, served bread elegantly with a silver fork, as he liked, and not with her fingers, as she loved to do, and chatted with perfect spontaneity of the things she knew would touch him — the cream ponies at the circus, the lady acrobats, the lovely weather, the approaching harvest.

And Andrew interposed: 'Nice straw there was in the ring. Just like heaps of snow.'

'We supplied it this morning!' Charles glowed. 'I went up with Catherine and took the order.'

'It was beautiful straw.'

Two words were enough. Charles pushed back his chair, charged his pipe, and behind the flapping of the match showed a pair of dreamy, satisfied eyes.

When shortly afterwards Andrew rose and said 'Good night,' he fixed her with a gaze which seemed to her enigmatical, burning and plainly asking something. Violent, excited tremors seized her as she looked at him. It was a shock to see him disappear.

A minute later, shutting the door hastily behind her, she was running after him, whispering up the dark stairs:

'Your candle, your candle.'

He appeared suddenly from above, like some one on a raised stage. A yellow, murky stream of light shone upwards into his face. 'Ah! yes, the light,' she heard him say and then he descended slowly, step by step, while she climbed upwards, until an arm's length divided them. The candlestick was shaking in her fingers. Her attitudes, her gestures, her manner of looking at him were all transformed. She noted, for some odd reason, a pleasant way he had of pursing up his lips and a half gold tooth which showed as he smiled down at her.

She too smiled as she paused on the stairs and gave him the candle, though she dare approach no nearer. Then as he bent down and took the candle he touched the orange-bud at her breast and said:

'Don't let it die.'

'No,' she said softly.

It seemed to her very beautiful to talk to him so.

'And you will call me in the morning?' he asked.

'I will call you,' she said, with delight.

ALL the following afternoon, in a long brooding seclusion in her bedroom, she lay thinking of him. Occasionally there reached her the low note of pigeons from the square, the sound of a thrush breaking a snail in the garden and the faint noise of a band from somewhere far away.

She knew that he was sitting under the trees, on the lawn, reading with Charles. She had a vivid picture of his face, having once tiptoed to the window and watched him from there. She remembered precisely the angle of his head, lowered slightly, as if watching something in the grass, and the way the shadows of the apple-leaves had darkened and softened it and the garden had given it a background of bright, dappled green.

In the bedroom, where the sun made hard, deep shadows, as if drawn across the walls and the counter-pane with a ruler, she felt by turns afraid of the emotion that face brought her and then infinitely happy that she had at last succeeded in securing for herself an ecstasy so intense and absorbing. Nothing of its kind had ever happened before, nothing to make her dote on the infinite details of any one face as if she were possessed, as if she had never before seen a face. It was all new to her in its intensity, its sweetness, its intricate and never-failing wonder, most of all in its moments of overpowering longing when she felt she must go again to the window and call down to him, regardless of everything:

'For God's sake come and talk to me. Come and be near me!'

She had her moments of quietness, also moments when she repeated tranquilly, yet assuredly: 'It's happened. I knew it, I expected it,' when she felt that nothing besides that one simple event had been needed to make her happy. She was not surprised at it. The only thing that set her wondering was that no one had noticed the difference in her and in that day, that she could still move and talk with all the attributes of a normal being, cherishing her new emotion as she might secretly have cherished the fragments of some dream too strange and wonderful to relate. And how was it, above all, that no one noticed her looking at him? Long ago she had learnt that she was not good at concealing emotions. And yet, today, bearing within her the essence of all that was most difficult, most incomprehensible and marvellous to bear, she had acted with an air of calm, unwavering detachment, deceiving everyone, sometimes deceiving even herself, into thinking that life had not changed for her.

In the bedroom, however, she brooded in the certain knowledge that all life was different. Its cold shapes, its solid outlines and unchanging proportions had been set shifting and quivering. She herself was some new, warm, trembling creature. The very way she tucked her hands under her face, withdrew them, pressed them to her mouth and put them back again was new to her.

'What shall we do? What will happen?' she thought.

She stretched back her arms and clutched the wooden rail of the bedstead behind her. She did not care what happened. Only now and then she felt that overwhelming desire for him to be near her, so near as to enable her to stretch out her arm, bring him even nearer and not release him until she had communicated unforgettably some part, at least, of her ecstasy and joy.

All the time she was absorbed in listening. The stillness brought everything, and when, shortly after three o'clock, she suddenly heard him go to his room, she heard everything, his feet on the stairs, on the landing, in the room next to hers. She felt in those moments that all she needed was to be able to go on listening. And then suddenly she thought:

'He's going, he's going.'

She scrambled up. Was that true? She shook out her skirt, went to the door and stood listening. She heard him hastily shut a drawer, move across the room and move back again. She felt her heart throbbing violently. In the silence she listened again.

Suddenly he came out. He was startled at seeing her. With an attempt at calmness and deliberation she said:

'So you are going?'

But her voice was only a whisper. He stood perfectly still, and as if not understanding what she had said remarked in a low voice:

'This is where you are, then?'

Suddenly she was frightened at herself, at the feeling of unutterable joy which suddenly mounted in her at the mere sound of his voice. Not knowing what to say or do, she clasped her hands under the neck of her dress and stared at him.

She was conscious only of thinking: 'He will understand, he will know what it means, he will understand.'

She began to tremble again and then, anxious that he should not see that trembling, made desperate efforts to remain tranquil. All the time he was looking at her with a strange, searching emphasis. She said nothing; did not even shake her head. Suddenly it occurred to her: 'What if I'm mistaken? What if he doesn't understand?'

A feeling of desperation overcame her, a feeling that she must explain to him at all costs the emotion over which she had brooded all afternoon.

'Why are you going so soon?' she managed to ask.

He did not answer.

'Why is it? Can't you tell me? Can't you tell me?' she repeated.

He remained silent, looking as if every line of her pale face, with the darkness of the passage behind and the light coming through the bedroom windows, hurt and unnerved him. And suddenly, unable to bear the tension of those warm, tense, silent moments any longer, she broke out:

'Tell me, come into the room and tell me.'

She began backing away from him. He appeared suddenly hesitant, afraid, and did not begin to follow her.

'Oh, do come. Only a moment,' she whispered.

'Listen, I want to tell you something.'

He looked at her suddenly in a way that was an agony and a pleasure to her, and which she felt also must have brought pleasure and agony to him.

'What is it?' she said.

She retreated a little more. He began following her. 'What is it? What is it?' she kept repeating.

On the bed lay her red shawl and abruptly for some unknown reason she picked it up and held it in front of herself and smiled faintly. The pleasure of that moment was gripping and wonderful. Then she felt that she had suddenly become certain of what he was about to say to her. It was as if she could see it shining clearly in his face, silent, enframed in the doorway.

'Listen, I want to tell you — ' he began suddenly saying again.

She half-opened her mouth, as if to say the words for him. Instead she formed a smile which hung there trembling, giving her an expression of glad expectancy.

He saw it and it seemed to arouse him, for he began suddenly murmuring: 'I love you, Cathy, Cathy, Cathy,' trembling and half-laughing as he said it all, using his hands to make odd, pitiful gestures, as if to make clear and emphatic the incomprehensible meaning of it all.

'As if I don't understand, as if I don't understand,' she kept thinking to herself.

She threw back her head and with short, breathless pauses he began giving her long kisses, and somehow it happened that she found herself against the bed-rail with his hands imprisoning her face and her whole being struggling with a strange, confused pleasure against an emotion she felt must overpower her and which did overpower her at length with its warmth and delight. And all the time she struggled also to speak, to utter one syllable by which he would know how she too had cherished and suffered that same emotion. The shawl slipped to the ground. And suddenly, like the shawl, she felt powerless to keep from falling and begged him in a low voice to hold her up, and he did so, and she existed at once in a state of dazed, trembling wonder, laughing and weeping at the same time, conscious only of the nearness of him and a vague desire for everything to remain like that for ever.

Presently they stood apart, looked at each other and began smiling. The vagueness of their smile only seemed to express more perfectly their emotions, their delight in each other. When they came together again his hand would press her breast and she would keep clasping and unclasping her hands, while he maintained a shy, prolonged look at some vague point between her brows and hair. They did not speak. Now and then, looking away from each other, their eyes would alight on the blue sky; some white cloud sailing across; the still, fretted edges of the apple trees and pears, through which odd patches of the sky were revealed when they moved in the wind and which reminded them faintly of a world which seemed already shadowy and far away.

How long that meeting lasted she did not know. Sometimes it seemed to her that for hours and hours he had simply stood holding her hands and gazing into her face. She remembered every moment of it and every moment was filled with a sense of delight which after he had departed made her restless and uneasy, then as it increased, reflective and silent. In the end it began to torture her so that she did everything apprehensively, with suffering, even fearing that she might die without seeing him again.

She began to take long walks alone. It was July: the weather was hot, thundery, oppressive, and in the woods, where she spent hours lying face to earth, wondering, dreaming, black clouds of little flies swarmed and troubled her. And in the same way myriads of thoughts kept up a ceaseless torment in her head. Life became bewildering in its exciting restlessness. Only rarely she fell into long, peaceful reflections, lying in the heavy, drooping grass with her eyes open, aware intensely of the movement and sound of everything, the thin singing of linnets, of woodpeckers laughing, the occasional call of a pheasant, and the rustling sound of branches swaying ceaselessly backwards and forwards in the hot stillness, like slow music, monotonous, yet comforting her.

There were moments of the clear, perfect realization of what had happened. Then she would think of him, his voice, his youth, rejoicing in everything she remembered his having said and done. She pictured him once again during the thunderstorm, the concert, in the garden, on the river and coming home from the circus. She recalled the far-off days when he had been at school, learning, she supposed, Latin and Greek, and she had not seen him except at long intervals, when he had scarcely spoken to her. She even fancied that possibly even in those days she had, unconsciously yet profoundly, felt some love for him.

She longed to see him again. She never reasoned on what their love, if they fostered it, might lead to, but thought of it only as an emotion, fresh, compelling and tender. It never seemed to her foolish or guilty, but only miraculous, incredible, a great wonder. She never thought: 'Shall I go away with him? What if Charles should know?'

She received a letter from him, entreating. 'Come and see me,' and not dreaming for a moment of the possible difficulties and consequences of such an act, wrote in half-frantic joy that she would meet him in Harkloe.

He wrote back: 'Not in Harkloe. At Olde, on the hill, outside. It's quieter and less noticeable. And the woods are beautiful there.'

It did not matter. She began to suffer suspense and agony in waiting. Something frequently made her tremble with alternate anguish and joy. For her absence on the day itself she managed to make excuses to Charles that deceived him completely. She arrived at the edge of the wood in the middle of the afternoon. In the quiet, solemn air some pigeons were circling lazily over. It was warm, hushed and languorous. She filled with happiness. And then at the sight of Andrew it seemed her whole being quietened down, ceased working for a moment or two, leaving her staring at him mutely and with wonder.

They entered the wood and walking into the heart of it sat down under a ring of young birch trees. There was a hush. The small, pale, delicate leaves of those trees made a curtain of soft, transparent green above them. She began peeling off the white bark of the birch trees, and let it fall into her lap. And solemnly, without speaking, as if it were to him the expression of something deep and beautiful, he watched her, while she now and then paused, let her gaze rest on him and then glanced away again.

Silent, naive, timid, they fell suddenly into a long embrace with each other. Her head became pressed against the white trunk of the birch tree. Some rings of bark loosened from her hands and all but one dropped among the others in her lap. The other did not fall and even ceased in a little while its soft quivering in her fingers. Their silence and stillness increased. From a thick forest of oak leaves a chaffinch flew down, explored the ground aimlessly about them and flew back again. On the edge of the wood some people went by in a cart, singing. But none of the sounds seemed to reach them. It seemed that all the time they must think of nothing else and exist for nothing else but that deep, silent happiness and wonder.

Suddenly they ceased embracing and she began laughing. She laughed at first silently, her eyes dancing, her face all happy ripples and curves, then with a sound that was soft, joyous and musical. She threw back her head still further so that the sounds might escape better.

He began to speak then. 'Why are you laughing?' he kept asking, 'Why do you keep laughing?'

She felt that he knew why she was laughing and did not answer. Instead she stretched out her hands, put them on his shoulders, then gradually raised them to his face and began touching his brow, hair, ears, eyes and mouth. And it seemed she had never known such a pure, deep delight as when touching him.

He seemed to know that she felt that delight. 'Ah, you are happy, you are happy!' he kept telling her.

She felt that all her life she had longed to hear just those words, to hear them spoken as he spoke them and in such a place. And it seemed to her that while he uttered them she must do nothing but sit still, watching the strong, yellow sunlight pouring through the oak leaves, slanting across the trunks, falling in broad, unbroken patches through the bare spaces, and that the sunlight was part of her happiness, playing on her life as it played on the leaves, the grass and the earth, enriching and transforming them.

When he became silent again she renewed her looks at him. His attitudes, his watchfulness, his silence and the depth of his still eyes, now doubly intense with the reflection of her own, moved her to whisper:

'How long have you waited for this?'

'I don't know,' he said softly, 'I can't tell you. It seems so long.'

And she became conscious then of no longer wanting to watch him, or the sunlight, or the green, hushed wood about them, but only to talk to him. They began talking. They talked a long time, at first timidly, hesitantly, as if not knowing what they wished to say, but after a little while, quickly, fearlessly, they began confessing their love, pouring out all the fears, hopes and desires they had cherished so long.

She sat upright. A spirit of intense, vital absorption possessed her. From her cheeks shone a soft flush of pink, as if they were of pure, milky glass with a flame within. She dazzled him. And he began suddenly telling her that she had always dazzled him and that she had moved him, often and often, to bewilderment and despair.

'I used to wonder if you would ever know,' he said. 'I used to feel it must be so plain in what I said and in my face and in everything I did. And now when you do know I can't realize it, I don't know even if you understand it all and if I ought to begin to explain all over again.'

'Don't explain,' she entreated. 'I know everything.'

'But before you came to see me today, and then before Sunday, did you know then?'

'I knew long enough ago.'

'What did you know?' he asked.

'I can't tell you. But it was terrible and glorious.'

THE following day was a troubled one. She felt she could not face Charles. She went to church. The service seemed long, artificial and dull, and for long moments she was preoccupied with Andrew's face as she had seen it in the wood. Everything seemed too vital and wonderful.

Returning home she sat on the doorstep, as she had seen countrywomen do, and nursed her chin in her hands. Before her the garden sparkled with sunlight, and on the nearest cherry tree, overhanging the wall, she could see the cherries were ripe. Presently she heard footsteps and Charles came in with a basketful.

She did not look up.

'Nothing the matter with you?' were his words, looking closely at her.

'Nothing whatever,' she whispered.

'Come, tell me. I know better.'

In desperation she hesitated, thought wildly and then complained of toothache.

'Ah! I will get you some cocaine on cotton-wool,' he said. He vanished, while she continued to sit there thinking of their relationship with bitterness and fear, feeling abject and miserable.

Suddenly something in the sunlight falling among the masses of green brought back to her the sweet, extraordinary idea that it was part of her happiness. Her face became radiant and her body seemed suddenly like a spray of leaves set trembling. Getting up she moved a foot or two away, then a little further and, still further, until the house was invisible. And all the time it seemed she must lift her arms up to the cherry trees, their dark, heavy masses of fruit and leaves and the turquoise sky, and whisper that she was happy, happy, happy.

When she returned to the house Charles stood holding the cotton-wool between his thumb and forefinger.

'Put it away,' she implored.

'But this toothache,' he reminded her.

'It's not toothache,' she said desperately. He tried to protest, but she left the room.

In the afternoon and evening she walked out of the town in the hope of meeting Andrew, but never saw him, and returned at sunset half-expecting that he had come to visit them by another way. He was not there. Charles and the Galloways were there, waiting for her.

Charles astonished her by excusing her before the others. 'She is not herself,' he remarked.

'I'm out of sorts,' she whispered.

'Play us something if you're like that, then,' they said.

And not knowing how else to ease the conflicting ache made by the personalities of those people and the memory of Andrew, she went to the piano and played two or three pieces. At the end she said, a trifle sadly: 'I'm sorry I've nothing new to play.'

'When you are in Harkloe you might think to get some new pieces to try,' Charles said.

'Perhaps I will,' was all she promised.

They had supper. She was troubled more than ever by her position. Something frequently set her trembling. A single phrase of Galloway's, 'In this country alone three thousand women die every year in childbirth', repeated itself, rolling backwards and forwards in her head like a stone.

And Charles told a joke which to her seemed grossly obscene, but at which everyone laughed, Charles himself most of all, going red in the face, choking, and finally coughing on to the tablecloth a piece of half-chewed salad resembling a lump of greenish phlegm.

'God, how awful! How awful!' she thought. Feeling ashamed, more than ever unhappy and desperate, she almost wept.

Later, going out into the garden, she thought with alternate grief and joy of Andrew, their love, the one extraordinarily beautiful day they had spent together, when they had found for the first time a pure, uninterrupted expression for their emotions, and life had seemed to her infinitely beautiful. Everywhere was wrapped in a warm, summer darkness. The cherry trees, stooping heavily down, seemed struggling to caress her. She leaned her head against a trunk and recalled the moment when it had been pressed softly against the birch tree. It was ecstasy. She prolonged it and the sky and the garden seemed to slip away into darkness.

Then, not having ceased thinking of Andrew for one moment, she went in and wrote a long, imploring letter to him. It was late when she finished it. Having finished it, she went to bed and lay thinking, at times dispassionately, at others desperately and with anguish, of all the ways in which, since it had become so agonizingly necessary, she could still go on living with Charles and yet deceive him.

PART THREE

ANDREW FOSTER's lodging, a room on the third floor of an eighteenth-century house, stood between a wine-and-spirit shop and a baker's. Opposite the door was a third-class restaurant where customers sat on high stools or at dirty tables with tops of imitation blue marble. As early as nine o'clock a smell of cooked herrings, chops and stewing tea began mingling with the aroma of fresh bread and wine. Further along a fishmonger in blue would sweep into the gutter fragments of ice, rank sawdust, and occasionally the red tail of a lobster. Between the restaurant and the fish-shop stood a small, tidy-looking shop painted red and white, bearing over the window the name *Goldoni*.

Goldoni's was kept by a little Italian, who looked like a Jew, and his wife. These two spoke bad but charming English and sold coffee, Parmesan, Gruyère, olives and white-wine vinegar. This shop had always attracted Catherine. She had first bought coffee there. The coffee had been excellent and had at once provided her with an excuse to say that at home, in that wretched little town, they could get nothing, a thing which for a week she emphasized and repeated in the presence of Charles. For a week also she got plain, ordinary food and lamented continually, 'What dull food I have to get!' She repeated that if only there had been exciting things to cook she would have been happy. And then, tentatively, she began to suggest buying food on market-days in Harkloe, asking Charles if they had ever, in all their lives, had coffee like that from Goldoni's? Even more tentatively and shrewdly she worked out, item by item, shilling by shilling, including the train-fare, what it would cost to shop in Harkloe. Finally, half-astonished at her own prescience, she read the list to Charles and explained everything in a breathless sing-song, childishly, artlessly, until it persuaded him.

Afterwards, each week, she wrote Andrew a letter of a string of strange, aromatic names, enclosed money and begged him shop for her. The very simplicity of it all was beguiling. On this errand Andrew one day walked out to Goldoni's. The sun beat down on him strongly. At the street-end only a solitary plane tree dropped a quivering green shade. Walking along he thought of woods on a hill-side, Catherine's body against his, its seductive scent, and a glittering canopy of leaves giving them cool, beneficent protection above.

And tiring of the hot street, he turned into a restaurant three doors from Goldoni's and ordered coffee. As the waiter turned away he stopped him, thought a moment, and changed the order to a glass of sherry.

Then, as he sat sipping it, looking out into the hot, narrow street, he suddenly remembered the trip to Germany he had taken a year before. This trip had lasted several months, and for the most part he had spent it in restaurants and *biergartens*, drinking un-limited lager and coffee. There had, of course, been women too — though in all those old, towered Rhenish towns, with the Rhine itself winding through a green gorge patterned with vineyards, and even in the country, among the peasants, where he had hardly under-stood a syllable of the *patois* they spoke, there had never been a woman like Catherine.

Sipping his sherry, drawing pleasant green and

yellow pictures in his mind, he re-lived all this. He thought also of Catherine, the passion he felt for her, and which she, liberally and warmly, in turn gave back to him. A picture of life as she lived it now, colourless, enervating, stagnant, rose up before him, and filled him with renewed impatience, while he saw Charles as a figure he had perhaps always hated — a dry, narrow, cautious mind that was revolting to him.

The thought of Catherine's love, on the other hand, warmed and tranquillized him. Like an inspiration he saw suddenly that if only she and the green vineyards of the Rhine could be interwoven life would assume fresh contour and joy. And longing suddenly to be with her, he all at once paid for his sherry and left. It was past two o'clock. In Goldoni's, while they were grinding coffee, he gazed absently at the piles of cheese, fairy sweetmeats and rows of white-wine vinegar and Italian wine, while thinking of her. The bottles of wine became fixed in his mind and at the last moment he suddenly bought a little flagon of Chianti. For no one else, he thought, as he hurried out, could he have done that. But for her — yes! because she liked wine, because she knew good wine when she drank it, and because it would make her happy.

He climbed to his room, flung himself on the old red divan under the window and waited for her. She generally arrived at half-past two. It was now twenty minutes past. Sunshine was just beginning to slant into the window. He rose, hid the wine he had bought, and gazed down into the street.

From time to time he fancied he heard footsteps. He constantly listened. Once he was seized with the preposterous idea that she had arrived, climbed up in silence, and was listening also outside the door. Cautiously he crossed to the door, waited breathlessly, and then flung it abruptly open.

She was not there. Clocks in the market-place struck half-past two. She still did not come. His agitation increased, growing easily more intense since he fancied that in that room she now left, each time, an impression of herself, some colour, some fragrance or disorder. Now to be without her seemed distressing.

Finally, at ten minutes to three, he heard footsteps. He waited for these footsteps to ascend. When they had ascended they stood still. He also remained still, aware that she had come.

Nearly a minute passed. It was as if they were listening to each other. Then the door opened and she came in.

She was weeping.

For a moment he was dumbfounded. Then that unexpected and incredible event made him run to her, seize her hands, and ask in a desperate voice:

'What's the matter? My God, what have you done? What has happened?'

But she was silent.

'What is it? What is it?' he repeated.

In the shaking of her head he foresaw the development of something unpleasant and tragic, such as a discovery of their love, and his hands trembled.

And then she suddenly burst out: 'Why didn't you come to the station and meet me? Why didn't you?'

'But did I promise to come?' he asked, astonished.

No, he hadn't promised, she said, still weeping.

He was mute.

'I only thought you might come,' she said. 'I felt it. All the way in the train I felt you'd be there.'

'But we said nothing.'

'I know, I know.'

'Then why are you crying?'

'I felt you'd be there,' she repeated wretchedly.

He stood still, not understanding perfectly the delicate nature of her disappointment and grief. Then he tried to comfort her, but she asked only to sit alone and still. She sat by the window, half in sunshine.

As he sat gazing at her his excitement about the Rhine and life there vanished. He sat and looked at her with wonder, feeling as if for the first time he had touched some very delicate spring in her emotions.

After a while he asked: 'Would you like to go out to the woods?'

There were no words, only a shake of the dark head in reply. She had not wept much, but her eyes were stained and her mute apathy, which even the sunshine did not dispel, disconcerted him.

They sat silent again, and this time a little longer.

Suddenly, not able to endure it, he impulsively rushed to her, pressed her head back on the faded red tapestry of the divan and in a confusion of words asked forgiveness. She appeared not to hear. But he continued, and suddenly it seemed, from a series of rapid shakes of the head, that she was listening. And not hesitating, not heeding her, he began telling her about the Rhine, the green vineyards, the peasants, the old, shadowy towns, the house where Beethoven had been born, with its cool courtyard and air of repose. And he pictured her as a peasant, with great boots, black stockings, voluminous petticoats and a spotted kerchief. He said he would take her to the forest, the dark, endless forest of birches and pines, still and patient, as if always waiting for something, and then to the towns, where they could sit, as he had done, in *bier-*

gartens, drinking coffee and lager, and afterwards hear opera at night.

In the midst of this he jumped up, searched and showed her the Chianti, saying:

'I know you'll like it. Shall we have some?'

She pushed him aside, however, and asked:

'What is the fare to Germany?'

He felt a little astonished, but he considered and replied: 'Perhaps three pounds.'

'How much would it cost to live there? Say for a week?'

'I can't say.'

'Tell me as near as you can.'

'I don't know.'

'Would it be expensive?'

'Perhaps.'

She was silent, moving her fingers, as if calculating something. The end of that silence and calculation was simply a slow shaking of her head.

'You can't run away with me. It's all dreams, it's quite impossible. What we gained we should suffer for — and God knows in any case we might suffer.'

'I never thought of going.'

'The idea's in your head, and if I had listened you'd have told me.'

'Yes, perhaps so,' he admitted slowly. 'But why do you object? Are you afraid?'

'I'm afraid of suffering,' she said. 'And there are practical reasons. Any kind of existence might look well from afar off; but when you become part of it, it's different. Not only that there's money. It's wretched and sordid — but have you got enough?'

'You know my grandfather left me a little,' was all he said.

'I haven't much,' she said. 'Together we couldn't manage more than two hundred. Yes. I'm practical now,' she conceded in quick tones. 'A year ago — even six months ago, it would have been different. I had all sorts of dreams then, and I was foolish and had no practical side to speak of — there was no need for one. Life was all laziness and I did nothing but play Chopin. Now it's different.'

Her voice quietened and ceased. Silent also, he sat and marvelled at the change in her. Now there were no tears, the tone of disappointed grief had gone, and she spoke as if bargaining over the cost of something.

To him this new figure presented difficulties and he longed for the old, passionate, dreamy one. But she appeared to have passed from that, to have shaken off that oppression, and had risen above him, sane, faintly incredulous and mature.

It was as if she had passed through too many experiences, so that he could never hope for her to reach up to him again, asking for comfort or pity.

It was this thought which made him ask, hopelessly:

'But isn't there a solution to the problem?'

'Yes, there is a solution, there's got to be,' she answered, perfectly consistent, 'but it's not that one.'

So she was determined, he thought. A little regretfully he turned away from her and gazed at the flagon and the glasses on the table. Pleasant and green pictures of the Rhine again began floating towards him. He longed to embrace them, to drink the wine and dispel his own sharp sense of frustration and her hard, practical mood. He wished he had never spoken of Germany.

He went towards the bottle and said: 'Have some wine now?'

She shook her head.

At this second disappointment, arising, as it seemed to him, from some cold, remote part of her, he sank suddenly into a chair. He stared for a moment at the sunshine, the glaring blue roofs of the town and the sky. And then suddenly he was conscious of her warm arms, breasts and face pressed strongly against him, some half-exotic perfume, and her clear, low and passionate voice filling the room with the unexpected words:

'Don't move, don't move. Only let me look at you.'

Those words soothed and touched him. Foolishly he went on his knees before the divan, stroking and kissing her.

ONE evening, as dusk was falling, she ran upstairs to his room with two bottles of wine. There were silver streaks of fresh rain on the window beneath which he sat watching her. Delicate, minute beads of it had fallen on her hair, so that it looked as if adorned with gauze, ready for a party.

She crossed to the table and set down the wine. Already a half-bottle of sherry stood there, with some flat, green glasses she had given him as a present a week before.

As she took off her things she talked about the wine, about the rain falling on her bare head, the peculiar habit Signor Goldoni possessed of never adding up one's bill correctly. She spoke in that curious way lovers sometimes have, whisperingly, intimately, half-selfishly, as if jealously anxious to keep secret every odd moment of their love.

When she had finished she crossed to the divan and sat by him. He began at once caressing and fondling her.

The furniture of the room was the same and was arranged in the same way as a fortnight before. Beside the divan there was the piano, now closed, and with some novels and a portfolio of Chopin *Études* belonging to Catherine heaped upon it; in the centre stood a table scattered with architect's plans, close to which the bottles were set; there was a bureau, also closed, and some chairs, underneath one of which had been thrust a number of pictures in frames. These pictures had once hung on the walls; in their place were now only two pictures, an etching of a peasant-scene in

Spain and a portrait of a famous Russian dancer who had visited the town a week before. The wallpaper had once been a fashionable light fawn colour with a cerise design; but it had faded, and now there were ugly square patches of the original shade where the pictures had hung. The room was not dirty, but it was not tidy. The bed, partially screened from view by curtains of rose chintz, was half in disorder. Through the half-open curtains was visible a narrow shelf on which stood a small plaster nude, over the head of the bed, on the spot where a devout Catholic might have placed the image of the Virgin Mary.

In arrangement the room, except for the pictures, was the same. In atmosphere, however, it had changed. There was now a scent of rose, mingled strongly with verbena, and the last of its formalities had gone, as if someone had carefully softened each corner.

Some dirty coffee-cups, a pot and a milk-jug had been hastily deposited by the fireplace. They had been there, unused, since Catherine's last visit. One cup was overturned. Some coffee grouts had been spilt, and the little remaining milk smelled sour.

Outside the rain fell in a pale, steady drizzle. In it there was the dreaminess of autumn, though it was still only August. Its sound on the panes was a soft, persistent murmur.

Catherine arched back her head and stared at the sky. She remained for some moments immobile, while Andrew sat watching her. Then after a moment he began kissing absorbedly a shadow on her throat, and from thence the lights and shadows of her face, kissing her lips the longest, most violently and most tenderly.

When it was over she sat up, and, as if it had given her inspiration and strength, seized him with her arms, dragged him madly down and returned his passion with overwhelming intensity. Then, relinquishing his lips, she uttered, 'God, God!' as if in agony. In response he held her fiercely and closely to him.

Once, during the next half-hour, she struggled up and poured out some wine; they drank three or four glasses rather quickly, as if in eagerness, panting a little. Then Andrew said suddenly:

'What a pity you can't get Rhine wine here.'

'Oh! don't talk about the Rhine,' she said.

'But it's good wine there, better than this. I've seen the vines growing and I've seen them make it. Everybody drinks wine there . . . Look here, I once had wine at the house of a blacksmith in the Rhine country, and — it's the honest truth — the man before him had a pipe laid from the cellar to the bed, so that he could drink at all hours of the day.'

'Nonsense.'

'It's the truth. He killed himself.'

'You've told me that before. I don't want to hear.'

'But it's amusing. You might listen.'

'I don't want to listen.'

With extraordinary force she suddenly declared: 'This German scheme is ridiculous, you know it is. I'm serious; I don't want everything to be ruined by some mad escapade. If we go away it's when we are certain of everything, not before.'

'Then we will go?'

'Of course.'

'Soon?'

'As soon as we're certain.'

'Certain of what?'

'There's only one thing to be certain of,' she declared vehemently.

133

'What's that?'

All this had been carried on hurriedly and warmly, with Catherine standing, occasionally making wild gestures over his head. Suddenly, with the words 'What's that?' this altercation ceased, she went down on her knees again and in a passionately earnest voice began reiterating, 'Listen to what I say!' gazing intently into his face, as if seeking to impress him with some deep, shattering truth.

He responded by caressing her. Again she reiterated, and again he responded in this way. After a moment she moved up to him, changing the words to, 'You understand, don't you; you understand?'

He said he did understand and again caressed her.

'What do you understand?' she whispered.

He shook his head. That was different. She knew, she really knew, she trusted him? If she ever had a moment of doubt she would tell him — save him the awful pain of discovery?

She got up and leaned over him. In stretching up his hands to her he ran them unexpectedly against her breasts and allowed his hands to remain for a fraction of a second touching them. She recoiled a little and, taking his hands gently, guided them to her shoulders. As she did this a passionate, hungry expression came over his face. He began breathing deeply. His eyes, turned away from the pale, rainy sky, seemed unduly sensuous and sombre. At his lips there was a faint trembling. Acutely she watched his dark, still face undergoing the agony of all this. Behind him the rain was blown from drooping clouds to soft drips on the glass. Inside it was quite silent. Abruptly she became aware of the faint noise of his hands slipping from her shoulders to her breast again; then that her breast was fondled, caressed to and fro, and lastly held as gently in his hands as in the grasp of a child. Her soft flesh responded to all this as the petal of a flower might respond to the touch of the feet of a bee. It was an ecstatic response, yet she never spoke, for she had an intuition that the time had not come for speech. Very dimly she realized that for certain moments there is no utterance complete enough. Once only she attempted to stop his constant caress, and raising her hands, touched his and made them desist, only longing for them to begin moving tenderly again a second after they had ceased. Her own hands fell away. The excited pressure of his fingers was renewed again. And now, surrendering to it, sinking down on the divan, she half closed her eyes, sighing profoundly at the last effort of physical struggle.

Abruptly a mental struggle began instead. Aware of the meaning of love, she told herself she knew the culmination of such an ecstasy. Nevertheless, she asked herself whether he knew, if for him it was some unknown joy, that ceaseless fondling, and if he knew what it awoke in her?

Then she heard him begin to mutter, as a sort of joyous entreaty, 'Cathy, Cathy, Cathy!'

Fixing her eyes on the sky, she saw an odd bluish-green shape become suspended there, motionless among racing clouds, it little by little became identified with her joy, then her fear, and finally her desire. The shape enlarged, became in turn beautiful, menacing, evanescent, as if part of a vision or a dream. Its spirit of passionate and threatening beauty assailed her like a perfume.

His cool, tender fingers travelled over her bosom. She heard him sigh. And it seemed to her like the sigh after an immense struggle, perhaps after pain, or like the sigh after childbirth or of heavy boughs. She conceived the strange, lovable idea of being a tree herself and of telling him, so that he might imagine the breasts he held were two ripe, unblemished fruits, which had ripened only after a great travail.

But she said nothing. Instead she bent forward, which made it easier for him to caress her. Now a furious, insufferable trembling took possession of her.

She wondered how long his caressing, his low murmur and this trembling could last, when suddenly her nervous sensibility reached some kind of crisis. She dropped her head to her breast, her lips apart, her expression like that of some animal's exhausted with running. In that way she saw that her breasts, held by his two hands, had expanded into shapes of a warm, magnificent and seductive beauty. Seeing them thus she felt afraid, as one may feel afraid at the sight of a bewildering loveliness.

Then he made a sign, as if of beseechment or understanding, without relinquishing her. Suddenly, as if recognizing only too perfectly the intense passion of this sign, she rose and backed away. Accidentally she upset the portfolio of Chopin *Études*, which fell with a clatter. A moment later she turned, ran and vanished among the faded pink drapery about the bed in the corner.

And lying there, expectant, trembling, she listened to his approach in a world subdued by twilight and hushed by the ceaseless and gentle spray of rain. She listened joyously, foreseeing for a single moment his excited clumsiness, his too hasty desire to possess and be satisfied, and the cool, still aftermath of it all.

CHAPTER THREE

By the middle of September they had become
passionately devoted. When she went to see him
in a wild storm of rain and leaves or under some
benign blue sky, the storm excited her and the sunshine
and the long slender shadows of afternoon filled her
with an eager, sensual warmth. At home, where pears
had already begun to drop heavily in frosty nights from
among copper leaves, she thought unceasingly of him.
By turns her love lay heavily, joyously or lightly upon
her. The big round berries of an Indian rose turned
deep orange, a bush of marjoram withered from frost.
An apple branch split off in a storm, and now sometimes
the garden looked desolate after rain. But by afternoon
the sun created soft magic illusions, as if spring had
come, and she had long, tender, illusory moods when
she dreamed and in fancy gave herself to him.

In actuality, apart from these dreams, she gave herself constantly, whenever he asked. He had known
other women, though she was never aware of this, and
gradually he taught her countless subtle and voluptuous
gestures; little acts from which she at first revolted, but
which she later accepted and performed with willing-
ness, then with some degree of pleasure, and finally with
a kind of exotic abandonment she could not suppress.

In return for these things he spent money on her, and
it became a kind of ritual for her to shut her eyes and
extend her hands for his 'See what God will send you'.
She never in all this failed in her old, shy, artless
delight.

He made her presents of things with enchanted

names. Aptly he chose the things which would suit her: a pair of black earrings with silver screws; a box of perfume; a casket of peaches ringed with green bay leaves and some Chinese ginger in a blue jar; a portrait of Chopin; an edition of his *Nocturnes* charmingly bound in vellum and with lettering of gold; and a box of ruby carnations, which in a moment of daring she took home and set in the drawing-room, telling Charles she had bought them in a moment of extravagance in order to please him. Then once she had a dream in which she fancied she was playing the piano with one hand while eating olives from a spoon with the other; she related it, and not long later he bought her a spoon of elegant silver. Lastly he set for her a seal of refined and enduring beauty on their love by a fragment of amber, clear, shiny and gold, which for long afterwards she wore between her maturing breasts, hanging invisibly there from a green string.

She in turn expressed her love less materially, acting always with an intense simplicity. She was simple in her excited acceptance of his gifts. Once, afraid that he might impoverish himself, she asked how he could afford such things, and then accepted the carelessly inscrutable shrug of his shoulders with simplicity too. Just as she knew nothing of the reasons for his once suspiciously leaving home, she cared nothing for the history of the days when she never saw him. He worked in the architect's office; he had friends; he loved her; and where she would have once been restless and discontent she became blissfully satisfied.

They would buy wine and drink it together in his room, sometimes by candle-light. With wine the delicate sensitiveness of their first love would change easily to something more profound, more jealous, and often in him to an ache that was ravenous and sensual. For her it created a blissful and dreamy state which in the end weakened her, so that she surrendered more easily to whatever he asked.

They had been drinking wine one night when a knock came. It startled them, and Catherine whispered excitedly while putting her dress straight. She did not know what she was whispering. Andrew implored her to be quiet as he went to the door.

Each time they were together they suffered fears, not always spoken, of an interruption. She feared Charles most. He was most afraid of being caught by his friends in the act of loving the woman already married to his brother.

There was an excited hush in consequence, until Andrew reached the door.

A man's voice began speaking.

Catherine could not catch the words. Little by little the door swung to and the aperture allowed her to see nothing. For some reason she carefully corked up the wine-bottle and hid it behind a chair before trying to listen again. All her steps were taken on tip-toes. Standing still, she tied the bow at her breast more securely, drank the last of her wine and eyed herself in the mirror. Her head throbbed.

The voices were raised.

'Don't come and bother me, please,' she heard Andrew say. 'It's a nuisance all the time. I can send it.'

'Well, send it, if you don't mind! I've got my returns to make. I'm not my own boss, you've got to remember.'

'I'll send it,' came an impatient mutter.

'Well, mind you do send it, that's all.'

'Didn't I say I'd send it?' The tone was angry. 'I'll send it tomorrow. I've got visitors at this moment.'

There came a muttered retort from the other. The door swung open a little, revealing Andrew with his back against it and an older man against the doorpost. He was the kind of man one sees at the sales of church dignitaries, retired captains and bankrupts. He assists the auctioneer, equally adept in cataloguing, moving a Queen Anne bureau or taking money; he is also sometimes the tout of insurance companies after a suspicious fire; he even makes an insurance book; but for what he deems a regular and honest occupation he collects rents in poorer districts, acting as the go-between for the tenants and the rich, comfortable, and always invisible property-owners, abusing and cheating the tenants and ingratiating himself in his monthly letters to the aristocracy.

This man was dressed in tight breeches, an old Norfolk jacket and cycling stockings. His face had the discreet pallor of servility, its harshness and sagacity mingled with something urbane and false.

She understood on seeing him that he had come about money.

'If it were my own business it would be different, sir,' he was saying to Andrew. 'But you see it's not my business. I don't collect rents for myself, sir. I only pay in to the landlady, sir, and she lives on the Riveeria and don't come to these parts above once in a blue moon.'

Catherine came nearer and looked into the dim outside passage.

'You see, miss,' he said on seeing her, 'rents that are behind get me into trouble. I don't lose nothing, leastways not money, but I get into trouble.'

She nodded. Then disturbed by the fact that Andrew owed money — for it was a maxim of Charles never to owe or lend — she asked:

'How much are the arrears? If you'll only tell me, I'll pay them now.'

The next moment she understood dimly that it was silly and tactless, and perhaps dangerous, to say this. And she knew why Andrew said at once:

'Nothing of the kind. It's not your business. What has to be paid will be paid by the end of the week, and I shall pay it.'

She kept silent. Andrew repeated in an offhand way his promise about money and the rent-collector went reluctantly.

Alone again they were silent for a time. When at length she asked, 'How long have you been in arrears with your rent?' he did not reply.

She was hurt by this silence, and by the fact that he would not confide in her. A puritanical, semi-middle-class upbringing had left her with the strictest ideas about debts, and she remembered often the pride with which her mother would declare: 'When we were in Bombay and your father died, we didn't owe a rupee.'

For the first time it occurred to her that Andrew might be making debts because of her. And now the room which had seemed so warm and gay and cosy with its German piano, its little etchings, its soft red divan and the fire shining on the green wine-glasses, produced on her an effect of moral uneasiness, as if for a variety of reasons she ought not to have been there. She wanted to say to him: 'Don't make debts. It's not necessary and they involve you so much'; and then again, reproaching herself: 'Don't spend money on me, so that you have nothing for other things, for things which are essential.' But she kept silent, and she knew she was silent because it might seem she was prying into his affairs, because she might seem puritanical, and because she loved and delighted in the presents he constantly bought her and did not want to cease accepting them.

She sat looking at his face. It was still and gloomy, but it seemed to her full of soft lights, soft, unexpected lines which made him adorable and forgivable. And suddenly she did begin saying, in a mild, tentative way:

'You don't owe money elsewhere, do you? You won't make debts because of me, will you?'

She tried to make this appear meek, even detached and unconcerned, though she was upset. But she could not do it, and suddenly she found herself touching and kissing him, whispering to him endearing and nonsensical things, as if he were a dog, interposing occasionally, as if it were part of a pantomime, 'You'll pay your debts, won't you? — promise you'll pay them?' and yet knowing at the same time that she was wrong and foolish and weak. She also knew that she ought to have been determined, refusing to accept his gifts, and even as an extremity quarrelling and parting with him in order not to put him into false positions.

But the gentle stroking of her hand never ceased; her voice expanded into warmer, as if more understanding, tones; and he too lost his gloomy, silent air, beginning to caress her in return, repeating idealistic and enchanting thoughts about his love for her in a vague, resplendent future.

And presently, the rent and the visit of the collector forgotten, they kissed, fell into long ecstatic embraces, and gazed at a portrait of a Russian dancer set on the German piano, saying to each other:

'Do you remember her — how beautifully she danced to the Prelude in A?'

NOT long later he suddenly discovered he had made debts to the amount of over twenty pounds. His meagre salary from the firm of architects did not last him long, and he began borrowing money, at first in small sums and, of course, with the strict resolution to repay quickly, then in larger sums, about which he made precisely the same resolution, but which he never kept.

By borrowing from one source he paid his rent. In order to pay a second debt he borrowed from another, and put the money on a racehorse. To his disgust and consternation the horse lost, and he was left with two debts instead of one.

He became wary of entering shops where he had once paid cash and had been treated civilly. The two hundred and fifty pounds legacy from his grandfather had utterly vanished, squandered for the most part in the trip to the Rhine. His family, with whom he was still in disgrace, would give him nothing, and he began to conjure schemes by which he could obtain a loan. Charles, for whom he had a sneering contempt, and to whom he sometimes secretly referred as 'the mean old bastard', 'the Jew', and 'the damned Shylock', was impossible. He was impossible, but a certain inherent meanness made him consider him. The same trait led him to consider Catherine. It was certain she would lend, or even give him the money. But he was afraid of the streak of practicality in her. She could be too insistent for him. And in the end he resorted to the safest and easiest scheme of the impecunious, and borrowed money from his friends.

He eased his conscience by paying a small debt. The remainder of the money, in some inexplicable way, vanished rapidly, and all he could see in return was a red scarf for Catherine. Bills came in, and he saw that one was for an item in April, which was now marked 'Urgent' and was accompanied by a sharp letter asking him to pay.

He resolved to pay. The same evening he went out with this intention he met an old friend, a University student who was about to go back to the University. Simultaneously they invited each other to drink; they drank all evening; after that he never thought of his debt again.

When Catherine came next day he suggested rather hastily they should go out to the woods. They would see the beech trees changing colour, he said, and the harvest being gathered in. To his relief, she consented.

'And not come back till dark?' he said.

That, too, pleased her, and he was satisfied. The town made him uneasy now.

They went by omnibus. White, billowy clouds floated over, and her black hair and red scarf waved gaily out in the wind. Often stronger gusts sprang up and flocks of leaves would fly out of the woods like brown linnets. She kept touching his hand gently and asking: 'I like you — do you know I like you?'

Secretly he was annoyed at this, but his quick nods were a source of great happiness to her.

In the woods she grew excited, clung to his neck, and in the end, as always, gave herself to him with generosity and delight. During those moments it seemed that the whole motion of the wood, its dancing boughs, leaves and yellow grasses, a red fly crawling on a burdock leaf and all the scurrying, whispering movements of little creatures running from cover to cover were aware of her love. And it seemed to her proper and beautiful that they should be aware.

And when they went on, she asked him:

'Do you remember how long you've been in love with me?'

He was silent, and emotions like doubt, fear and suspicion overtook her.

'The second of July,' she told him, falteringly, feeling as she said it like a young girl.

'Ah! yes, I remember,' he acknowledged.

But secretly she knew he did not remember. A spasm of unhappiness seized her.

'You're not in debt again, are you?' she asked, very earnestly.

'Not a halfpenny,' he declared, chewing some grains of corn he had threshed with his hands.

It was enough for her. In his face she saw something free, beautiful and ingenuous. And she never doubted him.

She began running about, catching leaves in her hands. Sometimes with naive gravity, she came and said, 'See what God will send you', and gave him a handful of berries or a scarlet mushroom. Through the open spaces of the trees cornfields shone in fitful sunshine and from what seemed a great distance the noise of wagons reached them.

But while she was open and light-hearted he only thought of his increasing debts, and had moments when he grew positively weary of the sound of her voice. He was greatly relieved when she said at last:

'Let's go down to the village and ask for tea.'

After tea they stood watching the wagons come and

go. On the shaft of one rode a boy in a blue smock. The men called to each other as they put up the sheaves. The wind blew moistly, driving across the sky dark blue clouds.

Everything seemed to her romantic and delightful.

'Ask if I can ride on a wagon,' she asked him.

Eventually he did so. A man in a check shirt and light yellow moleskins lifted her up bodily and she sat on the splash-board. She took off her hat and gave it to Andrew. The cart was loaded, the wheels rumbled and lurched over the stones. Her neck was pricked by the sharp butts of overhanging sheaves and she felt horns creeping like insects in her hair. Now and then she would stretch out her hand and touch the dark, glossy back of the horse.

As she sat there, swaying this way and that with the lurching of the cart, she felt gloriously happy. A sense of being elevated, of gazing down on the rest of the world, seized her and set her trembling. Yet she had time to notice minute details about her; the straws flying in her face, the horse, the sense of autumn, the thick, luxuriant smell of wheat, and barley and the odd sensation of moving steadily forward to meet the oncoming storm. She laughed at the driver in his blue shirt and moleskin trousers, his voice, the things he said, then at the horse, at Andrew walking alongside, at herself and at nothing. And she asked herself suddenly why, since she was so happy, she could not go on riding in that wagon, figuratively speaking, for ever, turning her back irrevocably on her former life?

Suddenly Andrew called: 'How long are you going to ride on that thing?' and too happy to analyse the tone of his voice, she replied:

'Only to the next field, just a little longer.'

But when the cart drew level with the field she never came down.

The cart went on to the village, where the houses and sheds looked transfigured by the grey, stormy light. The harness seemed to tinkle louder and more sharply in her ears. When she alighted she felt cramped and unsteady, and the sense of drifting endlessly forward to meet something still remained.

As they were walking out of the village he paused and asked: 'Will it be better to walk on or stay in the village until the storm passes on?'

'Let's walk on,' she said.

In the landscape began to come visible streaks of vivid green and brown. The clouds were a dark, heavy blue. In the distance a flock of birds, like a piece of black lace, drifted gracefully across the sky.

Now and then he would look upwards and say: 'It's going to rain. We've done the wrong thing, we ought to have waited.'

'Never mind, never mind. Think of the happiness,' was all she would say.

All the time she was filled with that strange intoxicating notion of drifting towards something, thinking of nothing except that she was alone and happy with him.

Then rain began falling.

They took shelter in a black, disused-looking barn with a broken door and a leaking roof. Pools of water gleamed in the floor and some rotten swedes were piled in one corner. It was the kind of place in which she had once heard him say it would be romantic to take shelter. He covered an old sack over the swedes and sat down and looked at his boots. She stood at the door and gazed at the falling rain. They were silent. Only now and then it seemed to her he grunted and murmured unintelligibly.

Once, as if everything had a great joy and significance for her, she sighed. Then, in a sort of panorama, all that had gone to make it so passed before her and impulsively she ran to him, threw herself on her knees and said breathlessly:

'Do you remember the thunderstorm?'

'What thunderstorm?'

'Oh! you remember: in the summer. It was dreadfully dark and I was frightened by the lightning. Then when it was all over I played you some Chopin.'

'When?' he asked.

'Oh! you remember, you can't have forgotten.' She stretched up her arms, let them rest on his shoulders and gazed into his face. He sat looking at the rain, slanting across earth and sky like heavy shadows in some picture, while she sat in a sort of dream, which the sound of rain, the smell of dampness and decay and the dark seclusion of the place helped to beautify and prolong.

Suddenly the rain hissed down tempestuously. With a quick, timid gesture of alarm she hid her face in his breast and put her arms round his neck. And it seemed to her suddenly sublime and wonderful that there was nothing to prevent her doing that, with all the resources of her strange, passionate nature, over and over again.

Some rain fell with a swift, icy splash on the hand about his neck. He stirred, stretched up his arm and gently removed her hand without a word. She stood up and began saying, as if it were a beautiful and imperative thing to say: 'When I rode on that wagon I was gloriously happy, and I thought how nice it would be to ride there always and not go back again. And why should we go back? What for? We belong to a different world.'

'Yes, but where are you going?'

'Where you like; only let's go.'

'Yes, but where? You keep saying, "Let's go, let's go," but where, where?'

'Don't make me miserable.'

She half-wept. He made an expression of tenderness and urged: 'Don't cry. There's no reason why you should.'

'No, I won't.'

A little later, the storm passing over, they departed. As they walked along the wet, gleaming road, with the smell of autumn and rain rising from all sides in the half-darkness, she kept giving strange, delicious shudders and laughing. And when he asked, 'What's the matter?' she said delightedly: 'It's the corn creeping about my neck and tickling me.'

And when, as they parted, she implored once again: 'Let's go. Think about it seriously. Think what it means. Promise me. It'll be all right, I know, I know,' it seemed to her that he half-turned away, glanced at the clock, and did not say 'I promise' earnestly or tenderly enough, as she would have liked.

And arriving home, she sat down and wrote a long, imploring letter full of that same thing: 'Take me away, take me away.'

And a little later, just as she felt she must sit down and weep and weep, Charles, drenched through, carrying a bag of dead pheasants, hares and partridges, came in, and with evident pleasure said:

'Look, there's a kill for you.'

THE following mid-week market-day Andrew had slipped away from his office for tea in the upstairs apartment of a little restaurant overlooking the dwindling market, where the windows were shaded from the brilliant day. The room was becoming crowded. As he chose his table and was making towards it, an uneasily familiar presence arrested him. For a second or two it was faintly irritating, then insistent, and at last exercised its stubborn power upon him completely. He turned and saw that Charles was busy watching him.

Their glances met jarringly. From Charles came a nod, its meaning studiously masked, in no sense committing him. He was not eating, which Andrew had time to notice while allowing his astonishment to subside. Then for a moment the question worried him: 'Shall I go and sit with him?' and some peculiar instinct seemed to insist that he must and that something would be gained from doing so. He had never known what lay in Charles's mind; if it were teeming with suspicions, only troubled, or perfectly innocent of his own affection for Catherine. He knew nothing, and the blankness troubled him. Now he felt it must be dispelled. Ignorance seemed to him more dangerous than risk. And he suddenly went over to Charles and held out his hand.

Charles shook it. The next moment the other felt that it was the very last course he should have taken: in itself it was unnatural, would provoke suspicions. He felt that thereafter he must be more guarded.

'Have you finished tea?' he asked.

'No, I am waiting for the girl,' was the answer.

There was, at any rate, no suspicion in these words. They were tinged with coolness and Charles's manner was stiff, no more.

'Which girl? If you could tell me, I can give my order too. You see, I haven't much time.'

'Yes, yes, of course. The girl in blue.'

Andrew as if by instinct searched for the inevitable sarcastic movement of the lips, but it was not there. He ordered his tea. Sitting down again, he was not quite sure of his own intentions. What was he about? Was it to fathom the depths of Charles's consciousness, his attitude to Catherine? Was it merely to throw dust in his eyes?

'A splendid day,' said Charles in a monotone.

Preoccupied, Andrew uttered some triviality in reply.

The tea arrived. Watching Charles's movements over the cups, the clumsy red fingers and thick wrists awakening comparison at once with his lover's graceful pallor, his attitude resolved itself. It was to throw aside all passivity, to become intensely and cleverly active, to discover at last what the penalties of indefinitely cherishing that lover were.

Charles, however, seemed disinclined to talk. He folded and ate bread-and-butter with persistent regularity, a coolness attaching itself to all his movements. Very rarely the eyes of the brothers met, and then antagonism stirred faintly, unsure of itself, driven by memory but restrained. Charles otherwise was inscrutable, giving nothing away, but missing nothing.

'Is business good?'

'Very fair.'

The compromise, the tone of voice, were both perfect. A certain irritability, part of that restless desire to know, to have things clear, took hold of Andrew. What did Charles think, what did he think? Had he the faintest glimmering? His innocence seemed immense, yet dare he question him directly? Had he the necessary fortitude, the strategy, the essential sangfroid to ask: 'How is Catherine?' Mentally he half rehearsed the tone of voice, striving for a discreetly innocuous manner, extremely difficult in its delicacy. It would not come. How could he treat her then — as a nonentity, a figure, as a distant friend, as if he had suddenly remembered her with genuine surprise? He did not know. And yet with increasing persistence it seemed he must know. His mind, burned by the question of it, refused all other thought and he found himself quivering on the verge of uttering her name.

'A macaroon?' interposed Charles unexpectedly and with a certain amiability.

'Thank you.' He took one, bit it, and then, staring with approval at the bitten remainder, let those words come without consideration:

'And how is Catherine?'

It was accomplished. Nothing could abolish it. He waited. Second by second it seemed to matter less that Catherine loved him than that Charles knew she had loved him. Secret, dark, covert, half-forbidden, that love would lose its glamour for him if discovered. Alert, he watched Charles's face, prepared for an answer dark and disguised with compromise and suspicion.

'She seems well,' said Charles, without haste.

He felt his thoughts, his perturbed desire for certainty, all become dead. 'She seems well.' What did that imply? Then, having for a moment a physical existence only, he watched Charles, unmoving, solemn, not responsive to the faintest impression. His pose had not even its old antagonism. He could not act or speak.

'At present she seems to be absorbed in the garden,' Charles went on. 'And then, of course, she's often here. She likes the town, too.'

Again that tremendous innocence, which it seemed might cover anything! What a fool he was! He felt breathless with astonishment at its deliberation and subtlety. His desire for enlightenment became effete; wildly he sought to change the subject before too late. But Charles repeated:

'Yes, she's often here. The shops attract her.'

He sat dumb. He felt as if waiting for a storm from which one cannot escape.

'Then also it's a change for her.'

'I suppose so.'

His tone, his stillness, expressed nothing. Fear, however, had careered along the passages of his mind, violated every chamber, all the secret and hidden places he had felt to be inviolate. He knew, he knew! He was racked by new torments at Charles's words. Nervously he drank a little tea, broke his macaroon in the effort to be calm.

Now neither warm nor cool, Charles became silent, steadily eating as before. His manner, too, expressed nothing. Andrew, bending forward to ask for tea, searched his face for the shadow of ironic triumph. He saw nothing — Charles did not reveal himself. The cunning of that negative pose struck him at once with great force — inscrutable and veiled, Charles, he thought, was waiting. And for what? No doubt he was perfectly aware of that too! And fear of every phase of the affair burst over him, until his mentality was an agonized mass of surging doubts, questionings, strident reproaches.

'Another macaroon?' asked Charles.

Almost fiercely he shook his head. That was too much!

The voice was suave, gentle — almost he thought his brother had cultivated the tone. He half took a glance at the clock. No, even though it was time, he would not go! And he watched Charles seize another macaroon with the thought that the crisis had come.

'I suppose you are still with the architects?' Charles asked in an impersonal way at that moment.

'Yes.'

'I suppose you like it?' Again the impersonal, waiting note.

'It's my work.' He too was waiting.

'Well, if you like it, let me tell you something. Will you?'

Abruptly they found themselves looking at each other, in every degree antipathic, opposed, but each intense.

'Yes?' He felt ready. At least he could be appreciative of the amusing irony.

'Be fair. Understand that, Andrew; do act straight,' Charles said entreatingly.

'To whom?' He was tense. 'What do you mean?'

'Everyone should be fair to his employer. All employment involves a moral contract, by man as much as master. There are, I grant you, times when . . . Only, listen, what I mean to say to you is — don't let it happen again. It's not worth the candle. It doesn't profit. I know.'

'What are you trying to say to me?'

'Just this — '

154

'Well?' He was trembling madly. What *did* he know?

'Try to be decent.' It was evidently painful for Charles to speak these words. 'Don't . . . you understand . . . don't go — don't go taking money again.'

They were silent. Charles had relaxed, as if the role of moral teacher had exhausted him.

Though relieved, relaxation, however, was not for the other even remotely possible. Intensely outraged at first, he felt that attitude gradually destroyed within him. It was ironical! — what irony! — what exasperating and grimly amusing irony! Charles the moralist, the elder brother, the preacher, the ingenuous saviour of his immortal soul — what could he do but laugh at him? Yet he still trembled, and moment by moment recalled his seconds of torture, that nervous and futile expectation of discovery.

'You will remember what I have said to you?' Charles suddenly asked.

He would remember! It would not pass! Slowly he nodded his head, glanced at the clock and said he must go. If only he could cease trembling!

'I will pay the bill,' Charles intimated, and he called the girl. 'Goodbye.' And he waved his hand, quite courteous and brotherly!

It was all over. Taking advantage of that expansive farewell, the other hastened off. But in the streets, at his office, going home in the golden evening, and in his room, while changing his clothes, the unspeakable torment of that interview refused to be allayed. The fear that had stormed his mind seemed to be celebrating increasingly its triumph. It intensified as he went over and over the scene itself. Once more the questions began: Did Charles know? How deep, how subtle, how comprehensive were his suspicions? How had he first come to suspect? And then again, why that waiting, watchful attitude, as if he *knew everything*? He called himself a fool, eating his evening meal rapidly, anxious for the calm evening air. When after supper he strolled by the river he was no calmer, however; he quivered spasmodically, guiltily remembering everything, calling himself a fool again. And now Catherine floated into his thoughts once more, bringing the inevitable remembrance that lately his passion grew quickly dispirited, he himself easily exhausted by her. Now the thought that he had less to lose at a greater risk almost maddened him. He tried to consider the situation logically, tranquilly. In what sense was she his possession? Only so much as he cherished her? Supposing he ceased to cherish her? Then it ceased to become an obligation to him, but devolved on her. Was that true? Yes, in a sense it was he only who was possessed. She it was who had always wished to possess, to love, to be immutable, not he. All that he had ever possessed was her beauty, her hair, her countenance, her body; but her soul, the inconceivably removed glory of her spirit, had eluded him. He had only a sensuous, a mortal contact with her. So that supposing he relinquished her, escaped? Supposing he did that, would anything be lost?

The sun sank. Dying, it gave out a daffodil light which scintillated on the water, tinted the willow-leaves, and made the sky an infinity of quiet silk.

Supposing he severed himself from her? Supposing he never saw her again?

A conscious answer never came. But he was afraid, he was unsure. Supposing he had given himself away, supposing, supposing? How did he know? Behind all

156

that brotherly moralizing, that amazing innocence, that dumb gravity — what was hidden? He shuddered. A family affair, his brother's wife! Hadn't he clear indications already that he was not a man of that sort? And he had forgotten himself! He, an egoist, to entangle himself in the wool of marital unhappiness! Weren't there other women? — she was built like another. And she herself — what had possessed her, what had she to gain? And now a recollection of her insistent, absorbed, almost pious devotion to him, the versatility, the tenacious faith of her love, repelled him. He felt himself succumbing without protest to its very quality of unselfish integrity, overborne by too great a burden of the absolute and the sublime.

He retraced his steps by the river. Women were promenading in the summer darkness, their fragrances floating after them. Lights shone from the dim architecture of the town.

'It must end,' he thought as he walked on. 'It will have to end.'

Nот long later, one half-cloudy, half-sunny day, she was sitting in his room waiting for him. To her astonishment the door had been locked and she had had to let herself in with the little duplicate key he had once given her. She sat playing with this key, rubbing her nails along its jagged, golden edges, thinking that today the cramped, disorderly space of the room was full of odd, acute little lovelinesses. She had kept her things on, a dove-grey hat and a coat with edgings of fur. Sometimes, wondering where he had gone, she listened with her head dropped to one side, and once, fancying she heard him ascend, went and lay on the divan, closing her eyes and listening, hoping that on entering he would kiss her there.

But the footsteps were not his. She relaxed. Waiting now was full of the wonder as to what could be keeping him. It was nearly three o'clock. Broad, slanting orange columns of sunshine had worked their way in at the window. Below, the streets were crowded and she leaned across and dreamily watched them.

She was not accustomed to waiting for him. Generally it had been that she ran up the stairs, suddenly whirled in and caught him reading or drawing. Today she had lived in anticipation, in a tremulous, tender heat about this meeting. All day her love had lain upon her with alternate anguish and joy. She had been conscious of a continual and more vibrant impulse to obey something, to respond to some more eloquent and insistent voice. She had woken up with a desire to be near him at once and, half awake, receive the softly powerful gesture of his body before drooping, childlike and satisfied, into another sleep.

Since then she had become calmer — it was the dead, English silence of the railway carriage which had at last accomplished it, she thought — and now, quite immobile at the window, it was as if she had conserved all her mature nervous anguish deep within her, with her disappointment and expectation and wonder.

Behind this immobility she drew pictures, in lavish colours, of the form their desire would take when he came. She took off her coat and hat, shaking herself very gently. Today she thought of their love as something extravagant. She wanted the most fantastic, the most protracted joy. She would talk of the Greeks and say that love must be drawn-out and sweet and divine. As she stretched out on the divan she imagined him with her. Her body seemed full of rhythmic beats, of singing pauses and sweet, joyful arpeggios.

She lay a little longer, thinking of this and toying no longer with the key, but with the curves of her breast. Then the chimes of half-past three aroused her.

The sudden realization of this prolonged absence of his perplexed her again. For a second time she looked out into the street. She saw nothing of him. The effect of this was to make her rummage among his books and plans, then among the music strewn over the piano, and lastly in the cupboard where he kept his clothes. She herself was a little uncertain of the purpose of all this; she thought of the possibility of a letter, a detail of some other appointment, that was all. What she was still certain about was that in another moment he would surely burst in, embrace her, tell her his regrets and be passionately full of love for her.

He did not come, however, and there was nothing in

159

his clothes to tell where he had gone. It had already occurred to her that he might have slipped out to Goldoni's. She locked the door and ran down to look for him. In the streets she never noticed the strips of sunshine, like yellow velvet, dropped carelessly here and there among the unfamiliar heads, and she was already flushed enough not to feel the sweet, childlike warmth of the air.

Goldoni's was empty. Signor Goldoni himself was busy grinding coffee, humming a little Italian song. Going on, she looked into the restaurant three doors away. There she could see a man eating fried fish, and a few people at early tea, but Andrew was not amongst them.

Puzzled, she walked back again. She walked slowly until she reached the stairs, then she ran up and bounded against the door. It was locked, however, and disappointedly she inserted her key and went in.

She sat preoccupied, thinking of all the conceivable misunderstandings and mistakes that might have kept him. Her dreaminess left her and she became practical. Instinctively her mind began to work in abrupt feminine leaps, often illogical, but progressive, leading her always to where he might be.

After waiting till nearly four she got up and, going slowly down, walked towards his office. Again she never noticed the pale sun, its quiet patterns on heads and buildings and trees, and the still, half spring-like air.

This time she hurried. His office was approached by some stone steps leading to a corridor, which in turn led to frosted-glass doors with bold, neat names. The corridor was dim, silent and full of disarming echoes. There was a smell of something bookish, obsolete and decaying, and through one of the doors, where the frost had been scratched off, she bent and saw red files, letter-presses, closed desks, and a clock which said ten past four.

All this overwhelmed her with a sense of desertion. To come to his door at last, screw its handle and find it fast against her, seemed a natural part of it all. She was not upset. Still only puzzled, she moved a little mechanically now, coming to the street and the odd, melting patches of sunshine without a definite purpose or thought.

This state of mind did not last long. And again she began thinking: 'Where is he? What is keeping him? Where else is there I can go and look for him?'

A year before she knew she could not have borne such questions. Her only gesture, perhaps, would have been to sit down and weep. Now, much more practical, and in any case afraid of the peculiar torment of waiting, she thought of a dozen places where he might conceivably be. She even included among them the prison and the hospital, fatalistically thinking, for perhaps a minute, of death. This passed, however. Inevitably she saw herself going back to the room to look for him.

She went back. Again the door was locked and again there was no sign of his having entered. All this she had half expected, but the shock on her was now greater; it set her trembling, perspiring a little; it lasted longer, producing for the first time a manner of slight desperation and restlessness. She began moving about the room, sitting in first one chair and then another. She picked up books and threw them down again. The piano was closed; she opened it, took one glance at the yellow keys, then shut it and went over to the bed. Touching the emerald and blue and rose of the eiderdown, she could not suppress a sudden thrill at its softness and at the thought that she might have been lying beneath it, pressing herself to him in a dream even more magically thrilling and painted.

From her first touch on the bed she was aware of the folly of it. The scent of sheets had its association; she suddenly recalled all his absurd, boyish gestures with her clothes; his sweet, delighted cries at his first vision of her; the way she had stretched perfectly still, as if sleeping, while he gazed and touched her pale-olive limbs.

She began to suffer for these moments of weakness. Her desperation grew, mounting and possessing her until, without tidying herself, she went out again.

Orange disks of sun burned in the high windows, but now there were heavier groups of cloud. The streets were already cool and dim. In deserted passages there was a rattle of dead, unseen leaves.

She hurried from corner to corner at random, not knowing where to look for him. Her mind now leapt beyond its practicalities, becoming a little fantastic, cradling secret and terrible notions. She walked as if in a hurry to reach somewhere, but always without knowing quite where she wished to go.

Gradually she found herself dismissing the probability of little things, seeing only something important and vital as his excuse for not having come. She began to feel, also, a little weary.

To the room she felt she could not return. She thought of the restaurant, and there, ordering a pot of China tea without milk, and refusing the pert 'Nothing to eat, miss?' of the waitress, she felt pinched, solemn and exhausted. While waiting for the tea to come she looked round at the munching heads with disinterest, knowing he was not among them. The teapot dripped golden pools on the marble; there was no strainer; the cups had ugly blue swallows with crimson breasts. She thought briefly of the tea she had once made for Andrew in the garden and of the old, red, forgotten shawl. That day she had seen herself climbing to a new pinnacle; and now she knew that she had climbed, had climbed beyond Charles and the street, even perhaps beyond Andrew also. Like all new emotional experiences, it left her isolated, and now, in the restaurant, with the forlorn tea and troubled by the agitation of his not having come, she was most oppressed by loneliness.

She sipped her tea. It was nearly five; lamps were winking out. She watched them with half-closed eyes while thinking of one problem and another. All the time she strove to drink, watch and consider calmly.

Suddenly she paid her bill and left.

Going straight to his room, she filled its dark emptiness with confused whispers of his name, the thin tinkle of the key thrown on the table. After this she sank down in a sort of collapse, breathing hard and listening. Then unable to bear the silent darkness, she got up and lighted first one blue candle, then another.

She saw at once that he had not been. She sat down, quite still, not protesting at this.

A long time passed. She was not aware of the extent of this time. She stilled herself into the erect immobility of the candles on the piano, without visible agitation or wearying or sinking.

This attitude lasted until seven o'clock had gone. By that time her fears had become like black clouds, incessantly appearing, never vanishing, but piling into a drab, unpleasant mass.

She had grown hungry also — a physical hunger with its numb, peculiar pain. But now she felt she could not face the street and the restaurant again. For a little while she bore her hunger; then she told herself that hunger was breeding fear, and that for the sake of fortitude she must eat.

In the cupboard she found oranges, cracknels and some wine. She ate an orange, swallowing quickly. The sharp, acid juice seemed to bite her throat. She began to eat greedily, walking backwards and forwards between the bed and the window. The room was cool and she lit the little gas-fire, warming herself at its columns of yellow and blue.

Presently she uncorked the wine and drank a little. It filled her breast with warm, searching spasms. Her body woke to its former need, to its craving for warmth, pleasure and excitement. As when she had stretched on the bed, she felt the necessity of being physically awakened and gratified. All day she had been conscious of this urgency; now she saw it becoming importunate and distressing. The realization of this made her struggle desperately to be calm. She looked steadily at the blue candles, their shadows, and the dark surface of the wine. Her head seemed full of gentle, dancing shapes and the sound of music, murmurous and far away.

She drank more wine, stretching supinely after each glass, waiting for its effect on her. The effect reminded her of the touch of an excited lover. For a while she liked this effect. She appreciated it, prolonging it and asking for nothing more.

Presently she discovered herself pouring out the last of the wine. Knowing there had been very little less than a bottleful, she watched the last slow, yellowish spots with astonishment.

'How much have I drunk?' she thought. 'Was there

as much as all that?' And then: 'I mustn't drink any more. I mustn't!'

This odd, determined attitude kept her still. The dancing in her head grew more rhythmic and more pronounced. She finished her wine at a single gulp.

Curiosity, five minutes later, would not let her rest. She must, she thought, see if there would be wine enough for him. She must! And if it were there she must set it out on the table. It was his wine.

She approached and opened the cupboard with peculiar swaying motions, discovering and clutching a second bottle with a low, delighted sigh. She set the slender, straw-bound flagon on the table, watching the still, golden reflections in the depths of blood-colour, weaving some rich, absurd and shapeless dream about it all.

Then she began drinking, gulping at the rough sourness of the wine eagerly, brushing her hair away from her damp, hot brow with her hands. She acted nervously, trying laboriously and with a queer, stupid pleasure to disentangle the fresh dreams from the old. All this she did in a difficult kind of twilight, sometimes exasperating, sometimes exciting, but never lessening. In the end she surrendered to it simply in order to obtain the relief following surrender. Behind it all lay a dim reproach, a distant and feeble question as to why she was doing these things. Then also there was the old, never-diminishing wonder about Andrew and the desire for him to come.

Sometimes she sank into apathy and thought he would never come. From her mind would emerge a dim muttering: 'Perhaps he's ill. Perhaps he's gone away. He grew ashamed.'

She walked unsteadily and heavily to and fro.

Suddenly she came upon a magazine he had been reading, an old illustrated German paper, with a photogravure cover of bottle-green. She picked it up and sank down and began perusing it. And she saw suddenly the Rhineland as he had drawn it for her, the summer vineyards, the river with its blue reflections, the groups of fat, pleasant, healthy-looking Germans sprawling in sunlight. It excited her. She turned over the pages quickly, realizing the pleasure that great river had once given him. And in her excitement she thought that if only he were with her she would revive that pleasure, stimulating him into taking her too.

As she looked at it now she saw no difficulties. She thought of their going at once, that very week. As to the money, she had long ago counted it and made it straight. There was enough, she thought — enough for so much of the future as she could see.

She was hot, perspiring. Lying on the divan, she loosened the bow at her breast while looking at the magazine with dull, flushed eyes.

In the magazine she came upon a picture of a group of sun-bathers, a man, a woman and a boy-child, ingenuous and free and laughing in their nakedness. She gazed at them with fixed but tremulous intensity. She thought of the man and woman, brown, divinely and softly shaped, as lovers — lovers of a perfect and understanding kind, lovers as she now wished Andrew and she could be. She thought also that if only he were with her she would, joyously but seriously, give herself to him with that same frank purity.

She got to her feet and walked across the room, laughing weakly in a sort of happy titter. She reached the bed. She was weak now and she sank on it, extending her hands in an odd, groping way. Then she put her face to it, sniffing it and at the same time letting her hands wander helplessly over the different patches of colour. The pleasure of everything was lessening now; there was instead a strange, many-coloured and often colourless pall upon everything, inflicting for some reason or other a burden, a pain on her. She seemed shut away from her joy and expectation, even from her reproaches, by all this. Very feebly, yet insistently, she wanted to weep.

She shed a few hot, difficult tears and lay still for a long time. Nothing happened. The stairs, the room, and even the night outside, seemed quite silent. And now she fell into a half-fatalistic, half-imbecile mood when she told herself he would never come.

A little later she got together her things, went downstairs and, finding it painful to walk even a few steps, stopped a cab and was driven to the station.

And at odd moments, feeling sick at her greediness for the wine, she would ask herself what imposed on her the necessity of doing these things?

TOWARDS nine o'clock that evening Andrew Foster came out of the first performance of a variety theatre. Overhead loomed a perfectly black sky and it was raining lightly. Below scrolls of silver mingled with red and gold and ran dissolving among passing vehicles and the dispersing audience. By the wall a black, half-drowned-looking string of people stood waiting for the second performance. Miniature rivers of rain were running down the painted posters bearing the faces and names of those who were performing. There were some clowns, two dancing girls, five acrobatic Japanese, a bass singer, some banjo-players and a conjurer. There rose a low hubbub of voices; while above the murmur echoed the shrill voices of newsboys shouting a robbery of jewels and an attempt on the life of Mussolini.

He kept as close to the middle of the crowd as possible. Umbrellas sprang up in all directions, affording a peculiar sense of protection. When the greater part of the crowd had dispersed, he sheltered with a body of people under an arcade, hanging his head a little, as if not wishing to be seen.

He had been in the town since nightfall. The afternoon he had spent in a little village, to which he had walked in order, ostensibly, to reconstruct a plan of a half-ruined monastery, of which a refectory, an immense black hearth, a gateway and a few monks' cells were still existing. Not far off lay a fishing-pond with an island of willows, where once upon a time monks had fished. It resembled a gigantic cup and saucer. The willows were fading and dropping leaves on the water. Between the ruins and the pond were scattered heaps of stone grown over by red sorrel and convolvulus.

After arriving there he had done a little measurement and calculation. Then, since it was merely an excuse for escaping from Catherine and the thought of his debts, he gave it up and began poking in the holes under the willows. He thought that perhaps a jack might come out, and it was pleasant to lie and watch the waving green weeds concealing the mystery of the gloomy depths.

Once he leaned over and saw his face reflected in the water. It was in reality a face bearing obvious weaknesses; its chin imperfectly moulded, the lips wide and loose until they stretched into an engaging smile. His eyes were deep, sensuous and attractive, and whenever he looked at his own face he felt a curious sense of pleasure. It was not the same pleasure he had once gained from gazing into Catherine's face, or into the face of his mother when a child. He had never known it in women, except in the face of a French girl he had once slept with in Marseilles, a dark, lovely, insinuating little wretch who had robbed him of a hundred francs before morning.

Yet, as he lay there gazing at his dark reflection in the fish-pond, he secretly knew that he would have gone back to the French girl as he so often came back to himself, simply for the sake of that rare, vain, inexplicable pleasure which imposed on him not a single moral obligation or responsibility.

In the past month he had become increasingly aware of something irksome in thinking of Catherine. She was becoming too persistent. There were increasing obligations. Two of her little blue envelopes often appeared in the post together. Her letters were long, abstract and wandering. The sentences lost themselves in each other. And he could not remember how often he had been bored or exasperated by the desperate, desperate tone of her love. 'My sweet one,' she would write, 'I'm desperate. Charles looked at me today as if he knew. Oh! if he really knows! I don't sleep well for thinking of it, and as soon as I wake in the morning my head aches terribly and I brood on it until I'm silly again.' She would call him endearing names, and at the end of the letter send him blessings.

At first he had liked those things. Now he asked himself why she foolishly addressed him as 'My sweet one', and continually blessed him?

Now also he was troubled by his meeting with Charles and his increasing debts made complications. The idea of a domestic scandal was more and more preposterous. And the Charles who had once seemed no more than a simple, harmless, purblind country merchant changed into a fearful and dangerous party in some unpleasant game.

It was a relief to have escaped from it all. He had no conscience and it never touched him to think that she was patiently or dejectedly waiting for him.

A sleepy red moth flew over the pond. The sun emerged and silvered the eddies he made. It was very pleasant to lie on one's belly and think of fishes, monks, life a thousand years ago, and forget women and money.

He idled among the ruins all afternoon. When he reached the village again a shadowiness had fallen; the sun was vanishing and the air was becoming cooler and mistier; some flocks of starlings flew over and there was a scent of damp and decay.

There was a shop where he might have tea. The shop was half-dark; an odour of freshly-baked cakes reached him. There appeared suddenly a young girl who asked him, 'What would you like?' in a thick, pleasant country voice. He spoke for cakes and tea to drink, and she asked him to follow her. In a second room, where it was warm, snug and nicely-scented, she looked pretty, bustling with the cups and spoons. He noted and admired, as he always did in women, her bust, her face, her arms, which were slender and quite beautiful, and then her hips, which were full of seduction and grace. He said something nice to her as she brought in his tea. Her thick voice induced in him a queer, sleepy desire to kiss her. She too seemed inclined to remain in the room, and they fell into conversation, a silly, warm, friendly conversation from which he discovered her name and her half-holiday. Then he kissed her and ran his fingers over her breast until she tittered.

He enjoyed it all. There were, no doubt, certain little refinements which she lacked, but he could teach her them. It would be pleasant to walk to the village and attempt it on dark evenings.

Under the arcade it was of her he thought and not of Catherine. Now when he thought of Catherine he felt simply bored, bored, bored.

And day after day, from that point, his boredom increased. Her long, tragic, appealing letters imploring an explanation of his absence failed to touch him. He no longer felt the urge to think of her tenderly, considerately, or even at all. Two letters seemed so silly, frantic and dramatic in their appeal that he could not finish them, but destroyed them with a sickened disgust, reproaching himself for ever having become entangled with a woman so odd and persistent in her affections. Then, little by little, he ceased to trouble about her.

He was troubled only by money.

CHAPTER EIGHT

THE ride in the cab had been like some bad, dark
dream to Catherine. Its blackness had been cut
sharply by sudden lights and beams of red and
gold that tinted the raindrops; shouted news of Mussolini and some winning horse; and at moments by dim,
awkward memories of some other ride in a cab, perhaps
a hansom, some relic of her childhood which now pushed
itself insistently into life again, leaving life something
between a dream, obscurely aggravating, and a conscious ache. And then the ride in the train: the empty
carriage, the white, shining washing-basin, and the
corner into which she had sunk exhausted, her hair
making an untidy imprint on the dark, vapoured glass
— these had all seemed part of the conflict of nightmare
and actuality.

For long intervals she shut her eyes, nursing herself,
feeling sick again. There were times when she realized
only hazily where she was.

The station emerged at last. She saw the booking-
clerk, pencil in mouth, crouching in the light beyond
the pigeon-hole. She felt the rain on her face, gave up
her ticket, and heard the engine shunting in darkness
far away.

In the avenue, her feet ploughing the wet piled
leaves, the clock striking half-past ten, she had her first
coherent thought. It was of Charles. She became aware
of him, not as she had been aware of Mussolini and the
cab and the dark world, but as in a picture, as in a portrait by flashlight, vivid, grotesque, yet realistic. She

thought at once, 'Will he suspect?' and a tremor of fear, like a brief gust of rain, swept through her. Then she became quiet again. Surely she had long ago learnt not to see the shape of fear till it matured?

He must have heard her approach to the house, for at the door he met her with entreaties and inquiries in a trembling voice.

'Where have you been? What is it? Were you taken ill? What is it?' he besought her.

'Let me sit down,' she said.

In the light, with the familiar chairs, the oval table, the photographs and pictures and newspapers, her mind acted with comparative coolness and order again.

She sat down. She judged it would be wiser to let him speak. Then suddenly, his expression between mistrust and fear, he began staring at her.

'What's the matter with you?'

She had to cry.

He seemed to speak with difficulty:

'Your face, your face,' he was crying.

'What's wrong?' she asked.

'It's strange.'

'How — strange?'

'Look at it,' was all he could say.

With difficulty she rose and looked in the mantelglass. His reasons for alarm were then obvious: she saw the face he saw, its eyes with their look of remoteness, as if driven into the head; the black, twisted skeins of hair hanging over the pale forehead and the cheeks with their smears of bright, fevered red. Her lips trembled in a kind of nervous dance, and she wore an air of strange sickness, faintly odious even to her as she stood watching.

Her brain, in the effort to conjure credible excuse

173

for all this, revolved frantically. She knew the time had gone when she could be sarcastically vague or rebuke him with indifference. Life had assumed a sternness, an inevitability, a reality; real also were its lapses and excitements and fears; sentimentally abstract illusions and sighs no longer existed. The very gleam of the gaslight in the ceiling had, against the memory of the candles and the darkness, a kind of unemotional sternness too.

Somehow she preserved equanimity. He looked puzzled, wondering, a little suspicious. She told herself frantically she would have to impress him.

In a weaker voice than before she murmured:

'I haven't been well.'

He glanced at her remote eyes, with their blue moonrings beginning to show beneath, but said nothing. She suffered a tremor. Now he seemed to her openly suspicious and incredulous.

'I fainted — I've been sick,' she said.

He was slow in answering:

'Yes, I can see. Where were you sick? — how? Where have you been all this time?'

His manner was inquisitous, dogged, more firmly practical than ever her own could be. The old air of pomposity, that went so well with the ridiculous collar, had vanished. With an abrupt start she told herself that behind it all was some warped, ugly notion of what had been going on.

'I've been terribly sick,' she murmured again.

'Where?' he insisted.

She told him desperately then: 'At Andrew's. It was the only place where I could go.'

'And what could he do for you?'

A little ashamed, she said:

'He gave me some brandy and I rested there.'

'Ah! did you see a doctor?'

'Yes, I've seen a doctor.'

'Well, what did he say?'

'Nothing — nothing very startling.'

'Aren't you going to tell me?'

'Yes, of course.'

There was silence; and then an abrupt:

'Well, what was it?'

His face looked rigid, purposeful and determined against a waving background of yellow light. Shutting him out for a moment, she whispered:

'Not now; afterwards, afterwards.'

There was a note of desperation in her voice. His sobriety, however, never wavered. Now it seemed to her that by the very way his hands hung, white, still, complacent, he suspected something.

She told herself she was not afraid of him. He could be complacent, but not subtle; she doubted if he could use complacency to deceive her. On the other hand, for her to deceive him, to keep him in a state of uncertainty till morning might be easy.

'Get me some cold water,' she begged.

He went away. While he had gone she suddenly perceived the intricacy of everything, the complication, how near everything verged on calamity. She felt wretched, and at moments she recalled waiting in Andrew's room, the unhappiness, her sickness, the humiliation, the despair. She even saw with perfect clearness for the first time what it all meant to her; she understood that long absence. It was the end; it was finished. Nevertheless, she was still aware that it would grieve and infuriate her; that she would spend days of torment, struggling desperately to complete the change from one phase of life to another, walking about that long, bare, ruined garden without satisfaction or hope. And she saw once again a return of the darknesses which had once troubled her, the loneliness, the little grievous, gnawing thoughts wearing her away.

Everything was still precious, however, still a dream, the end of which, whenever it came, she told herself she would endure alone, without him, without the presence of suspicion and fear.

And suddenly, when he returned, gave her the water and asked:

'What was the matter with you? What made you come over like that?' she spread out her hands in desperate, abrupt, inspired deception and said softly:

'Surely you know?'

He shook his head. 'No; what is it, then?' he asked.

She did not answer.

'What is it, then?' he repeated. 'What is it the doctor told you?'

Now for some reason or other it was not difficult for her to look at him. And gazing up into his dull, puzzled face, it seemed suddenly that she was telling the truth, pitying him.

She said softly: 'I'm going to have a child. Yes, listen, listen — it's true.'

He was silent. For a moment she wondered fearfully if that low, quick, invidious statement had failed to touch him; if he had still no faith or belief in her. Then she glanced quickly up at him.. His mouth had fallen a little apart, his eyes had grown large and soft, bringing about the sort of expression she would never have dreamed possible for him, an expression of joy, pedestrian, shy, unexalting, yet in its sudden profundity transforming him. She saw his lips move with perfect ingenuousness: 'A baby?' She nodded. Once again that expression of joy governed him. It prompted him to touch her, to a smile in which she read pride and forgiveness. It was pitiable, but it elevated him, leaving her a little guilty, a little sorrowful, but still adamant and desperate, sensible enough to know that to confess would not have converted it all.

She shut her eyes, and then, hearing him murmur: 'How nice, lovely, lovely,' half-persuaded herself of the truth of it all. To his brief, absurd gestures of pride and delight, his quick, awkward fumbling with her hands, she responded with a brief, weak smile, unable to look at him.

He gave her water, took off her clothes and held a sponge against her brow.

Her response to all this was serene, impassive; her conscience never asserted itself, as if lost or destroyed in some remote past; she no longer suffered in fear of him. Only now and then some calm, phlegmatic sense of satisfaction filled her — the dull expression of her cheap, simple triumph over him, egotistical, feminine, composing and gratifying her.

CHAPTER NINE

CHARLES FOSTER had fallen asleep on the settle in the room facing the garden that Sunday afternoon. The pale sunshine over his face, the noise of some children playing under the bare limes, and of Catherine moving to and fro in the room above had not disturbed him. He had slept a long time. Then, when he woke, it seemed cold, and he felt unrefreshed and depleted.

He shivered and lay looking stupidly at his reposeful belly while he wiped his hand across his mouth. The long shaft of pale gold sunlight had swung beyond reach of him like a sail. The fire was dead. Already the room had begun to be inhabited by little darknesses.

He listened. The noise of Catherine and the children had ceased. He listened for the wave of sound breaking from an open door, a late blue-fly, the clatter of spoon on china, the whir of a gas-flame under the kettle in the kitchen. Nothing came; the house reposed, and Charles relapsed again, his thoughts unexpectedly vivid, crossed in a bright pattern, a strange mixture of memories of a pheasant he had killed in the rain, as dead as a nail at the first barrel, an article on Liberal land-policy in the paper that morning, and lastly Catherine's strange home-coming, his suspicion, and the coming of her child.

Jubilantly his thought leaped forward to the future. He became joyous because of his hope in Catherine. From this day forward she was changed; for eight months more she was a little petticoat divinity. Soon he would write to his mother and see the midwife; and then go to his friends, perhaps a little proudly, a little ostentatiously, informing them that he had a son.

Suddenly, once again, he shivered. This shiver prolonged itself; shook his vitals and left him stretched gasping on the couch with a pain in his side. The pain was gnawing, pinching, ridiculous, like the stitch after running. His head was a little fuddled, too, in a dull, heavy, unpleasant way, as if he had smelt of poppies. Presently the pain ceased. But now the reiteration of the shivering was more frequent, resembling the rippling of a sharp cold tide up and down his body.

All this alarmed and tried him by its suddenness. He was a healthy man and instinctively his resistance was determined and strong. He swelled his chest, clenched his teeth and breathed hard, accompanying all this by the repeated utterance:

'I can't afford to be ill. I can't afford it, I can't afford it.'

But after five minutes of this he was only weaker. Now his thoughts of the pheasant in the rain, Catherine's wild face and his delight in what she had told him of her child were only confused parts of a chaotic struggling. To separate and clarify them he attempted to struggle upward. He raised himself on his elbows. The garden, with its leafy ruins and sad drenched masses of summer flowers watched over by the stiff, unfrozen red of solitary dahlias, seemed only a chimera, a grotesque, revolving dream. He attempted to quieten all this, to affix certain objects: the sundial; a square of broken green glass in a frame; a Blenheim orange fallen and lodged in a fork of its tree. This became like some absurd game, at which he failed wretchedly, as if his eye had grown feeble and dim, and which he gave up at length with a sudden, backward fall and a groan.

A minute later he was trying to call in a hoarse voice Catherine's name. His voice was only a whisper.

He had a little qualm as to the wisdom of calling as he lay panting. 'Perhaps in her condition that's not wise — not right.' He reproached himself. Rather blindly and mechanically he repeated to himself some maxim about the thought of others; then a shivering annihilated this, submerging him also with his chill, tomb-like dampness. A moment later he was whispering again:

'Catherine! I wonder where she is? Catherine! Where is she, where is she?'

He lay still, exhausted, in pain, and as in the beginning, listening for her.

Upstairs in the room with its view of the garden, a view through naked boughs to frosted flowers, red, yellow and copper ruins of things that had once been fresh, perfumed and beautiful, Catherine had been writing. On the bed lay a little shell-covered box, a red bank book, and a bundle of letters, the string of which she had not untied. The writing covered a square of paper no bigger than her hand.

She sat up with a start from these calculations of money and interest — calculations she had already done many times — as she heard Charles's voice.

She also listened a moment. The house was silent.

'Do you want anything?' she called.

There was no answer.

She called again: 'Do you want anything?'

Receiving no answer even then, she called a third time and a fourth time, and then, a little impatiently, opened the door. At that moment he uttered another groan.

She ran downstairs. Sitting upright, pale and

quivering, he had a look of bewilderment on his face as if he had been struck by an invisible force.

A little bewildered also, she murmured: 'What is the matter with you? Why are you like this? Tell me, tell me.'

He could not answer.

'Charles, Charles!' she beseeched.

The loll of his head was grotesque and doll-like; she noticed also an unusual thing — he had unloosened his collar. She spoke to him again, but he was silent, though struggling and anxious, as if he wished to tell her something.

'You're ill. What is it? How long have you been sitting like this?'

He was gasping, so that she thought: 'He's ill; it's dangerous!'

Something in his suppressed agony and motionlessness aggravated that thought. She felt her heart throbbing. With a sigh he leaned back again.

And then, inconsequently, came the recollection that once, in her childhood, when she had fallen faint, someone had chafed the soles of her feet. Stupidly, and conscious of her stupidity, she began unlacing his shoes; then peeling the thick black socks away. His feet were ugly, flat, and too long for the shoes he wore, the toes misshapen, clawing downwards and disfigured by hard yellow marks the corns had made.

She began rubbing his feet with her hands. They were cold. It was all a little repulsive to her: the chill, wrinkled flesh, like a toad's, the sharp grey nails and the sour odour of sweat, pungent and lingering.

He seemed to become in those moments more than ever an object, not for her pity, but for her scorn, her abhorrence, for all that was worst in her. Mental suffering had sharpened her perceptions and destroyed her illusions; now she saw him as the mean, noxious influence taking away her pity, her delicacy, that spirit which warmed and elevated and beautified her. With his feet in her hands she felt for one moment servile and ugly. The movement of her hands became mechanical, signifying how infinitesimal her faith had become.

He ended all this by asking for something to help him.

'Brandy,' he murmured.

'Where is the flask?'

'In the pocket of my shooting-coat.'

'Are you in pain?' She became a little desperate again, letting his feet fall. 'Tell me! What shall I do? Tell me!'

'Yes,' he whispered.

She relinquished him altogether and ran suddenly to look for the brandy. 'In the kitchen,' she heard him say. The shooting-jacket, hung over the back of the chair, was rain-sodden, patches of wet marking the lining and the pocket containing the brandy.

She returned. Then, for the first time, at the sight of his white, staring face, it occurred to her that it was the doctor he needed, and she ran for him.

CHAPTER TEN

A WEEK passed. Coming downstairs one morning, she paused to look at herself in the heavy bronze mirror hanging at the foot of the stairs. Her eyes were big and sleepy. The cheeks, having no colour except a faint creamish-grey, reminiscent of the colour of old lace, and a purple, half-moon shaped mark like a little bruise above each bone, startled her a little. Out of her apathy came the faintest change of expression before, with her slippers shuffling and the sleeves of her loose red dressing-gown hanging perfectly still at her side, she went slowly on.

In the breakfast-room it was silent. The blind had been drawn up and through the plum branches nailed above the window and the soft mist rising no higher than the heads of the cherry trees the sun was diffusing into the room ripe yellow light.

There reached her an aroma of coffee. Someone, a woman, was moving about in the kitchen. Catherine, after a moment, went and spoke to her, saying 'Good morning' in a low, expressionless voice.

The woman turned. She was Charles's mother, closely resembling him, her face having that same unmistakable construction, the low forehead, the dark, urbane-looking brows, the nose a little haughty, the lips ostentatious and fussy. She wore continually an air of capability and importance, crowned by an ugly cameo brooch at the neck of her blouse. She also said 'Good morning', and then asked, quickly:

'Have you been in to him?'

She shook her head and said, 'No.'

183

'You'd better not. He seemed quieter when I left him.'

Catherine turned away and sat down. Ever since Sunday, when she had run suddenly for the doctor, Charles had been ill. The disease, pneumonia, had reached its seventh day. Evidently his mother had been awake with him all night. Standing on the table a fragment of the candle she had burnt made Catherine recall the half-dark, oppressive room, the quickened breathing, the handkerchief with which, from time to time, the reddish, tenacious spittle would have to be wiped from his lips. She thought also of the atmosphere of care, strained watching, fear of delirium and death.

She sat thinking of this until his mother entered, bringing the coffee. Then she asked in a quiet voice:

'When will the doctor come?'

'About ten.'

'How does he seem this morning?'

'You can't tell. He's asleep now. Take coffee?'

She nodded, and then drank a little coffee without milk, not eating anything.

'Aren't you going to have milk?' she was asked.

'Not with coffee.'

'You should have milk. It's better.'

Without answering she stared up through the window, and for one moment it seemed as if Charles were speaking to her. She recalled that for four mornings now she had asked these questions, had been answered in the same way, and had finally been told to have milk in her coffee. She felt she could endure it no longer.

Depression came over her, not so much at the thought of Charles and of death, as at the change in things. About her the world had increased in quietness and solemnity, bringing sometimes an ominous, expectant air, in which the walls and passages and rooms would give up fresh sounds — the rustle of strange skirts, feet running stealthily upstairs, the click of a shutting door, and even sometimes a groan. Often in the passage below a leaf would start, blowing with a dead, scratching sound along the skirting-board, and come to rest in some remote, dark corner, bringing unendurable silence.

As she sat stirring her coffee, trying not to notice his mother, she remembered the change outside too. Bright and dowdy, the leaves of the Virginia creeper, frozen off their stalks, had buried the flower-beds, falling softly on the grass, scraping harshly on paths and window-sills. The grass had been left long and shaggy. And crushing the last flowers, leaving no trace as to which had once been stock or columbine, purple or gold, giant or shy, rain had come in prolonged misty storms, printing red and yellow stains on the stone.

In the house itself, the drawing-room clock, black marble with a pink and golden face, a wedding-present, wound up assiduously and unfailingly by Charles each Sunday, had stopped at ten past three; and the barometer in the hall, which he had never forgotten to tap meticulously with his right forefinger morning after morning, stood with its indicator where he had left it, while the hand had receded.

It seemed as if in her something had been neglected, destroyed or taken away. Often she beseeched that it might end, miraculously, unexpectedly. Always she felt miserable, knowing that if it ended it would end remorselessly, without glamour or pity.

She let her coffee grow cold. Made by his mother it seemed insipid, tasting as if of stale tobacco. If only she could make her own coffee again!

Later, going out to buy vegetables, she felt a faint sense of relief at having escaped from the house. Once it had seemed only dull and boring to live here. Now, faced with a hundred complications, of illness, death, change, all that had passed between her and Andrew, life there seemed an oppression, embittering and warping her. With bitterness she remembered the tranquil sunshine of that Sunday afternoon when she had added up her money, thinking of Germany and of Andrew, unable to believe she would see him no more. And ever since, waiting with a kind of stubborn faith for a word from him, she had seen it thus. Over and over again she had told herself she knew men. She knew their weaknesses. She knew also that he would come, would write to her. Some day her life would pass through that revolution she had so often hoped for, painful, perhaps terrible, but bringing her happiness at last.

At times during Charles's illness, it was as if she had seen the beginning of that revolution. Often it was as if he must die. Often she had wished for this also. Then the thought that that mature, ecstatic and delicious love of hers could be utterly free again would fill her with suffering and delight.

Slowly crossing the square, she came to the shops and peered into them. Magically the mist had dispersed and the sun was beginning to dry the wet, scattered leaves. In the cool, still autumnal air was a scent of rain.

At a greengrocer's she entered and bought vegetables. In the shop was a strong, friendly smell of onions, potatoes and dry earth. Dropping greens and beetroot into her fish-basket, the woman suddenly looked up to ask:

'How is your husband, excuse my asking?'

She did not know this woman. Giving a little start, she replied, touched and bewildered by this solicitude:

'There's not much change in him. We're waiting. Everything depends on today.'

Later, going into other shops, other people asked that same thing, always people he knew only slightly or not at all. Sometimes she was embarrassed, sometimes strangely touched, so that she could hardly reply.

Walking homeward again she felt a sense of reproach stir in her. Where was her pity? she asked herself. Why was she so mean and indifferent? Once she had been all warmth, and once someone had said that her voice sounded lovely and pure, like a linnet's, when she laughed. But now she never laughed. Her lips had fallen, drawn into a short, thin line, and looked cold and spiritless, never opening except to make utterances expressing her disillusionment and apathy.

Suddenly, as she came near the home, she stopped reproaching herself and brightened. The change was visible in her face. Her eyes became spirited. It was as if, struck by some vision out of a remote past, she had become reassured and happy.

She went into the house quickly. Voices were audible, and suddenly someone called:

'Mrs. Foster! Mrs. Foster!'

She ran into the breakfast-room. Galloway and his wife were there; Mrs. Galloway had called. As she said, 'Did you call me?' she saw Charles's mother appear, and knowing then it was she they had wanted, felt rebuked and awkward.

'Are there any letters for me?' she asked falteringly.

There were none.

It was as if someone had struck her. Reduced to a

state of moroseness again, she tried with composure to wait for the doctor to come. A quarter to ten boomed forth. She sat in the room where the black marble clock had stopped, feeling that at the slightest touch something in her might cease working also. Quite suddenly her face had assumed its old expression again — passionless, morbid, and without warning she was reflecting in a dull way about Andrew and her infidelity, seeing it all by a slow, difficult process, as if through some machine that had long since grown obsolete and ridiculous. She herself felt a little worn-out and absurd too. Something had robbed her of strength of will, her power to resist despondent things. It seemed as if she were living mentally, spiritually and even bodily, a passive life, driven slowly backward into some existence even more moody, craven and without hope.

It struck ten o'clock. From the steeple towards which she often looked with dreamy joy the notes came somnolently, with a cavernous echo. Between the chimes and the first stroke was an immense pause, in which she had often listened breathlessly, but which now disarmed and frightened her. The clock struck at last, a pigeon wheeled off, and slowly from west to east of the sky passed a white, feathery cloud.

Hearing the doctor come at last, twenty minutes late, and go upstairs, her heart began beating heavily. Then, Mrs. Foster and Galloway having crept up too, she went and stood at the foot of the stairs, listening and waiting for them to descend again. As to going up herself, she had not the heart; her courage was like a thin flag, dropping and dying. She told herself she could wait; she would hear everything, the doctor would speak to her.

The hall with its bright rainbow mosaic shone like

an altar floor, cleansed and pure. Today there were no leaves, no rustlings; so there was a silence which seemed appalling and deathly as she waited.

A door opened at last, letting a grey, misty streak of light across the stairs. Galloway and the doctor, emerging, began to descend, talking together. As she waited she felt half-guilty, half-afraid, as if she were a child again, with sickness, and the doctor about to examine her.

Galloway, as he came down, was showing the doctor a paper. She knew that paper. A graph, drawn carefully in red and violet ink, its lines neat, the up and downs resembling some sharp, scrupulous range of hills, it had been drawn to illustrate the fluctuation in Charles's fever and respiration since the first day. The chemist was proud of the achievement. She heard him discussing in a low, earnest, important voice to the doctor.

'Very much disturbed . . .' she heard him say, 'remarkable tenacity . . . the pulse I did not take, but the rest . . . you see . . . there, I only wait for the pre-critical rise. . . .'

She understood nothing.

They descended. The chemist, folding his graph with important care, passed her with a dry, inscrutable smile. Backing away, she stood against the wall.

The doctor beckoned her.

He was a tall, fair, cultured-looking man, with a Scottish accent and a low voice. Sometimes he forgot himself and called her 'Lassie'.

'The crisis may come at any time,' he said softly. 'You understand that?'

'Yes.' She nodded, as if she did understand.

Without warning he began to talk to her, speaking

189

in a low, detached voice, sometimes hardly audible to her, but always by its cultured sympathetic tone impressing and touching her.

'If you feel the strain and would like a nurse,' he said, 'I will have no difficulty. Don't be unhappy, and if you want anything, just come for me. That's right. Take rest. You'll not be the only lassie with her husband on her wee hands.'

He smiled. She felt at once touched, gazing at him with a sort of sad thankfulness, as if she had been infinitely comforted.

At the door he paused, turned, and whispered:

'I will come in again just after noon. And take no heed of that gey, meddling fool with his graph, will you?'

She smiled, feeling more than ever as if a child again. This smile, remaining, transfigured her and there returned to her a visible gladness.

Then, very slowly, she went upstairs to Charles. She entered silently and sat down, feeling like a trespasser.

Charles lay flat in bed, his right hip raised a little, one arm disarranging the red and yellow coverlet. His face was turned away from her. He was quite still, though she could hear his breathing, quick and harsh, resembling the moan of an imprisoned fly. For an inconceivable time she sat watching him. The morning sunshine, entering at the window, made a pale triangle of gold in one corner, falling on a picture of Cromwell the Protector ordering away the bauble, a picture which Charles had always loved, and then on a chest of drawers, on which stood the little box with the pinkish-green shells and edging of mother-of-pearl, a half-burnt candle, some medicine bottles, and Charles's watch, unwound and silent, with its chain at its side.

Except for those bottles and the immobile figure of Charles himself, the room looked normal to her. Here and there a little dust had gathered, now disclosed by the sunshine, nothing more. Through the window she could see the fruit trees as they swayed to and fro, shining with the night's wetness, against the clear blue sky. About the sky itself there was a gentleness, a soft, profound tranquillity. She stretched out her hands and let them rest in the sunshine. It was warm, as if the sun were newborn, as if winter were still far away.

She went suddenly and stood over him. His face was blue and shrunken. There oozed from his lips a reddish spittle, like the juice of a berry. She looked at him without malice, without shrinking, almost with resignation, as if with the secret thought that he was about to pass irrevocably beyond whatever petty dislike or fear she might have conceived for him.

He stirred as she stood over him.

'I'm here with you,' she said at once.

Immediately, as she spoke, a sense of falsity seized her. Secretly she began to revile herself, conjuring for herself low, horrible names, pitiless and remorseless in her self-contempt. She saw herself as in a grotesque mirror, maligning herself for lying and duplicity, for what she saw now as adultery, for an existence of selfish madness from which already the glamour had begun to fade.

While she did this he appeared to watch her. Evidently he had not been asleep, but only stupefied. The stupor had made his eyes profoundly sombre, so that now they seemed as if veiled by a thin, discoloured web. By some intuition she read in them the beginnings of a delirious imbecility.

Picking up a handkerchief, already stained with

191

patches of dirty orange, she wiped his lips. He emitted
a dull murmur.

At first incoherent, meaning nothing, this sound
grew presently into words, and little by little she
divined from odd irrelevant snatches that his mind
was revolving desperately about one thing — some
event which had impressed or delighted him, or made
him afraid.

'Be quiet; you must be quiet,' she said.

He let escape some murmur about herself and about
a child.

Recalling abruptly what she had told him, and of
how that odd, mute joy had seemed to transcend him,
she understood him then. So he remembered! — she
had impressed him! And suddenly, unable to ignore or
resist it, she felt herself flooded by pity, by shame, and
by the deep, persistent reproach of it all.

'Why did you do it? Oh! my God, why that sort of
lie?'

Her sense of loathing and self-contempt increased.
Now the sunshine and the profoundly sweet beauty of
the soft sky seemed to change. In the room the odour
of drugs and sickness grew intolerable. She remembered Hands — Hands's dirty house, his children, for
whom she had had so deep a contempt that they had
dragged him down — his sick-room, the apex of the
lovely, sunny triangle in the spider's-web, his long,
despairing look at her, that look which had struck her
so surely and poignantly as a prophecy of death. She
felt pity, remorse and terror struggling in her. Then,
feeling that she must weep, that she could endure that
low mumbling about the child no more, she ran out,
descending suddenly into the breakfast-room, crying in
a sort of whispered shriek:

'He's delirious, he's delirious. Someone go up to him!'

Old Mrs. Foster, with Galloway and his wife, were sitting about the table, drinking a glass of cowslip wine. Galloway, in his large, confident way, had been explaining his red and violet graph to them.

Her sudden coming upset him. Everyone leapt up. Old Mrs. Foster darted her hands towards the bottle and pressed in the cork, holding it securely there as she listened. The chemist's wife turned pale. Galloway himself, making a sudden gesture of capability, tipped over his glass, so that across the immaculate graph ran a yellow stream, blotting out the violet and red. Exasperated, he whipped out his handkerchief, murmuring, 'most unfortunate, most unfortunate', while making frantic dabs, finally seizing the paper and pouring the remaining wine with extreme care into the glass again.

Catherine herself could only repeat, 'Go up to him, someone! Please go up to him.'

His mother vanished with a faint cry. Flapping his graph, and at last calling on his wife to expose it to dry in the sun, Galloway followed her.

Sitting down, she closed her eyes, shaking her head to all Mrs. Galloway's entreaties.

For a time it was as if she were ill herself. Sounds became distorted, the nearness of things deceptive. Feet circled about her, though no one came. A bell rang, and close to her hand danced a silver spoon in a glass. Running away, the feet left a strange silence; she had abrupt rude dreams throughout which Andrew's face, elusive and mocking, roamed just beyond reach of her.

When she aroused she felt clearer, and a voice was quick to tell her:

'He's a little easier. The doctor is here.'

It was Galloway who spoke, having run down to dry his graph and to mark, if possible, the latest reading for temperature.

She watched him blotting and wiping the stained paper. He made at last a mark with a pencil and, coming to her, pointed it out to her.

'The crisis,' he said softly.

Nodding, she got to her feet. Not knowing how to bear the stifling throbs in her head, she went to the door. In contrast the world now seemed full of sharp, dazzling lights, and her thoughts were each like some swift, minute surgical operation performed with exactitude on her weaknesses — her fear, her lying, her deception and that senseless, passionate craving for Andrew.

She thought of Andrew. What had seemed confused, incredible and difficult to understand became suddenly comprehensible. She accepted all at once the imperfection in his love, even the fact that he no longer wanted her. It induced in her an extraordinary calm — a bitter, adamant calm.

During the next two or three hours she went about under the influence of that emotion. She would smile twistedly to herself. Again and again she told herself that Charles's illness, Andrew's silence, the coming and going of people, and even that absurd graph, meant but one thing: it was finished. She felt herself succumbing to the weight of these things, to the slow, remorseless fall of a thousand events, like straws, individually minute, collectively immense, bearing down on her now with enormous strength. Once she would have been afraid of them. Now she waited passively. Her reproaches ceased, and she ceased also to think of Andrew with that sad, forgiving tenderness which she had once preserved for him without knowing why, with that profound wonder out of which had sometimes sprung some delighted gesture of joy.

Gradually the house quietened. Galloway went back to his shop, his wife followed him, and all became silent. At odd moments there came over her the sweet, extraordinary feeling that nothing had happened.

Then for a few moments she went to see Charles again. A candle was burning and his mother was nursing him. It seemed to her she read in his pale, tired face: 'I know how it is for you. I understand. Don't grieve. I shall manage.'

Tears sprang to her eyes. Half feeling that he was about to die, she felt poignantly sorry for him, wondering what she would do alone, where she would go, who would care for her. The darkness and silence of the stairs grew terrible as she descended.

It was two o'clock in the morning when Galloway, waving his graph and shaking with excitement, woke her to say that the temperature had dropped and that there was hope again.

She had fallen asleep with her head in her hands on the table. Some pages of an unfinished letter to Andrew were scattered about and a lamp was burning.

WINTER came, and again Charles Foster, having recovered, walked through the garden each morning for his long white office that was so pungent of corn and clover. Once more the barometer in the hall was set meticulously according to its pointer of blue steel and the clock of black marble and a pink face had begun its perfectly measured and discreet tick again, gaining exactly seven minutes from Sunday to Sunday.

There had come a trim normality to the house again. The signs of illness had vanished. By degrees had crept back its peculiar silence, no longer ominous or terrifying, but the silence of a well-ordered and perfect tranquillity. Only the woman who now and then slipped in or out of the black front door seemed not quite part of it all, entering or emerging with an incongruous haste which set the door-knocker hammering brassily, filling the street with chattering echoes.

In another way she herself had recognized the incongruity of her presence there. She had grown fretful again. Her face had never recovered its soft, happy light, the cheeks were still thin, and the eyes reflected things darkly, as in a turgid pool. It seemed as if she worried a great deal and that the worrying left its mark on her face. Only rarely her face expressed a singular beauty of an introspective and half-conscious kind, with her head bent forward, her eyes regarding dreamily and fixedly the triangle of dark amber reposing between her breasts on its green string.

She thought constantly and in varying moods of

196

Andrew. She had heard nothing, not a word. Succumbing at last to a desire to see him again, she caught the train to Harkloe one afternoon, the same train she had always taken.

The day was gloomy; there had been no sunshine. Coming up from the river white mists shrouded the street that once, bright and snug, had been a carolling-ground for birds in the sunshine. It muffled the chime of bells, screened the heads of the limes and the fruit trees, and poured a black, unreflective dampness on the stone pavements. It caused also the lights in the bank at the street-end to be lighted that afternoon at two and the blinds to be circumspectly drawn by three. By the same hour the chemist's also was illuminated, its phials of emerald and red and blue having an air of warmth and glamour in the gloom. Behind them, as she passed, the chemist himself sat dispensing prescriptions. He pressed his soft, fat kneecaps gently against the drawer in which, long since, the graph of Charles Foster's temperature had been deposited and forgotten.

In the fog the train crawled slowly, wearying her, and arrived late. She walked quickly straight to Andrew's rooms, hardly knowing what she should say or do if she found him there.

As of old, the street, the dark stairs with broken banisters and the door on which someone had once scrawled a doggerel verse seemed friendly towards her. At the same time she trembled as she ascended. She knocked at the door and stood waiting.

There was no answer. Again she knocked. The same result and an empty kind of silence expanding all echoes as she wrenched the knob induced in her a feeling of relief, as if some terrible experience had been averted.

Descending, she passed through a mood when, her

truly sensible curiosity deadened and her fears increased again, she no longer wanted to see him. She thought of resigning herself as for months she had resigned herself to the fact of his silence and apathy. 'I will go back,' she thought. She had already discovered within herself an extraordinary, unsuspected and tenacious courage. She felt it would serve again. All her feminine resources came together in an effort to make convincing the thought that she could exist without this meeting. It would be painful. Possibly it would be useless too. But she never convinced herself, and making her way across the gloomy market-place a moment or two later, she felt again she must speak to him, thinking of him with that quiet, half-melancholy air that was like the background of a dream.

She made her way to his office. The sight of the corridor with its bold, frosted names and confusion of doors made her tremble again. A girl passed her with a pile of unstamped letters, another with a pen in her mouth. They vanished, very smart creatures, taking no notice of her, and she felt like an intruder.

She knocked at last at the glass door of Messrs. Willett & Simpson, architects specializing at good profit in the erection of red-brick, six-roomed houses, saved only from the deadliness of prisons by shrubberies (for which Messrs. Willett & Simpson made no specification), and tabernacles devoted to the preaching of a beautiful and distorted gospel and the glorification of omniscient God (to whom Messrs. Willett & Simpson were not affiliated).

A short, thick-set clerk answered her knock, and she asked:

'May I speak to Mr. Foster?'

He regarded her with eyes that blinked stolidly, as if

under orders to blink thus, and then asked if she would wait a moment.

To this she responded by a mute nod. Her heart pounded like an old mill. Still she did not know what she would do or say to Andrew when he came.

Presently she heard approaching footsteps, stood stock-still with the notion that she alone of all earth was the one thing not revolving and swerving madly, and looked fixedly forward.

The short, thick-set man appeared again, blinking tirelessly.

'Will you come in?' she heard him say.

She followed him, accepting first an invitation to sit in a broken office chair and then to pass through the glass door in the far corner of the room, with a sense between elation and fear.

Someone remarked at once: 'Good afternoon. Take a chair, will you?'

It took her a second or two to realize that it was not Andrew who had spoken. More passed before she discovered that he was not even in the room.

The man who had spoken did not even resemble him, and her illusions vanished hastily. Her puzzled and frightened attitude intensified as she regarded his face, the gross-looking front of a low, anthropoid head stuck on his big shoulders as awkwardly as in a child's figure of clay. The body itself was even more gross, bulging over the framework of the chair in which he sprawled. He did not even look like an architect, but rather like a publican grown too indolent for his occupation and mummified by some odd chance in this revolving office chair. A glass of whisky stood at his side, and when he turned to her there struck her an incredibly vile, rank odour.

'It was Mr. Foster I wanted to see,' she said.

The figure sat poking the interior of a dirty nostril, sniffing a little. She waited, increasingly ill at ease. He sniffed more. She had an insane thought that at any moment he might spit at her. At length, however, he regarded her intently and said, without haste:

'He isn't with us.'

Instantly he enlarged upon this by adding, in a less guarded way:

'He left us a month ago.'

She never moved. The effect on her was sudden and dazzling, leaving her a little as if paralysed.

With conscious effort the figure locked its greasy blue fingers together, smiled at first an inscrutable but later a faintly malignant smile, and becoming grave again, shook his head.

'Yes, he left us a month ago. Must be a month — yes, a month this following Friday, because if I remember rightly it was pay-day. Yes, quite a month ago.'

It was as if she had been lured into that close, smug office to hear a sermon. But she remained quite still, not asking or even thinking of the obvious questions, 'Where has he gone? Why did he go?' as if expecting sooner or later to hear these details.

The voice droned on. It, too, seemed as if half-mummified — a dry, thick voice without timbre or beauty.

'We have been expecting someone might call,' he said. 'I'm glad you came, very glad,' he added, looking up at her. 'You are his sister?' he inquired.

Having no wish to excite his curiosity and feeling in a sense that what he asked was true, she nodded.

'Ah!' He unlocked his fingers, took a drink of whisky

and gasped rather loud. The atmosphere of the room became increasingly revolting to her.

The voice droned on again: 'I'm sorry this happened, but I expect you know him. Gay young dog, I fancy. Hadn't he been abroad and so on? Mind you, we liked him well enough, we got on well; but he robbed us, and you can't alter that, can you? Yes, he robbed us under our very noses. I've heard since he was somewhat behind with his rent, too, but that's no concern of mine. That may be only a matter of shillings.

'At the same time' — the sentences became confused and disjointed — 'I grant you we ought to have been sharper — trusted him too much, no doubt — of course we didn't take action — what say? — oh! — It's expensive — more than we could afford to risk. Yes, there was some woman, I fancy. He liked the women. You, being his sister, wouldn't be blind to that.'

It struck her as being all the insane rambling of somebody purposely devilish. Surely he was sitting there deliberately maligning the character of that boy? She could not believe it otherwise. It was all grotesque and vulgar. The monstrous, 'Yes, he robbed us under our very noses,' seemed in itself a crime against him, against her own delicate and precious image of him. She wanted to get up and defend him against this. She felt that if only she could have risen and expressed herself clearly and touchingly on that point it would have been enough. Surely no one would have been dense or impossible enough to disbelieve her: she knew him, his temperament, his faults, his little idiosyncrasies, his odd vicissitudes. She saw him as warm and generous, passionate often to a point of weakness, but always genuine. That there should have been any other conception than this, or that she should have been blind to some palpable fault in him, seemed preposterous. She had loved him; she had given herself to him; she believed in him as certainly as she felt that fragment of dark, cool amber resting against her heavy breasts on its loose silk string.

But she said nothing. Why attempt it? It was a libel; she firmly believed that. The figure in the chair grew more than ever like some monstrous, impervious god, and she felt that Mr. Willett or Mr. Simpson, whoever he was, would never believe her — would differ with her always — would scorn her.

She felt a moment of triumph, secure in the knowledge of all this, and then asked:

'Do you know where he has gone?'

In answer came a repetition of the inscrutable smile, changing to a malignant one, and thence to a sort of ironic gravity as he said to her:

'Naturally we're not aware of that.'

Swiftly, at this, she rose. As she stood there erect, dignified, and feeling as if an outrage had been perpetrated on her personal vanity by having listened to his fantastic vulgarity so long, he said:

'I'm sure you feel it as much as we do.'

She stood in perfect silence. The rapid, agitated click of a typewriter reached her from behind an adjoining door. He heaved himself to his feet.

'You understand we shan't take action,' he remarked again. 'Cost us more than the twenty pounds he took away.'

'Twenty pounds.'

It was a statement, expressionless, a mere colourless echo of his words.

'Roughly speaking.'

Quite suddenly she said: 'I shall send it to you.'

'My dear young woman — ' he began.

'I beg of you to let me send it.' She was really imperative.

'I assure you he's not worth it. It's foolish, there was some woman at the bottom of it; don't shoulder his debts for him! Come, listen to me — well, if you believe in him like that, if it's natural you should feel an obligation about him in some way — well. . . .'

But she never heard the end of this. The room had already grown painful and distressing to her, and the man himself a thousand times more distressing and repugnant.

She hurried out in a state of great emotion. Her sense of outrage seemed in these moments predominant. Outside darkness had fallen, but now all the lamps were burning, so that the misty air was a riot of little soft, amber-coloured haloes. Beneath her feet the pavements were dull black mirrors over which she skimmed warily.

The insistent repetition of certain words during all this time was like an odd catechism. 'He robbed us under our very noses — there was some woman, I fancy; he liked the women — I'm sure you feel it as much as we do.'

It was too painful. Not until she sank into the corner of the railway carriage did it cease to be a catechism and begin to bear resemblance to fact. Then sobriety and fortitude came to her quite suddenly and with a strange clarity of vision. To accept the fact of what had passed from the lips of that gross creature in the chair would never be possible — yet incredulity could not go on for ever. It was neither revelation nor logic which took her to the heart of the matter at last. Intuition it resembled faintly, while being actually fatalistic — as if she had long before secretly known that such an event, such a moment, would come to pass inevitably.

The train crawled slowly, whistling with a sound like a wail at each little white gate and bridge in the darkness. Her head made a dark and fantastic imprint over the wet glass, and her eyes were closed, so that she saw nothing.

She asked herself repeatedly: 'Is it true? Could such a thing be true? Oh! could it be true?'

There were many things she had never known about him, but she was able to recall suddenly the evening when she had first discovered his arrears of rent. Had he ever fulfilled that promise to her? She could not, of course, ever know. There was a darkness already over some part of him — a dense and implacable screen which it seemed to her quite hopeless ever to dream of rending.

Gradually, however, this did not seem to matter. The question, 'Is it true?' came at once too imperative and too realistic to remain unanswered. She turned her head to and fro, as children do in a feverish sleep, revealing a face paler than Charles's own had been in those still, candle-glowing nights when she had watched him. The question racked her. She had suspected and feared many things — illness, faint-heartedness, indifference, infidelity — but this solution of his silence had never before tormented her.

The train crawled painfully up out of the mist and ran along a level ridge before running down to the river valley. Some immense smelting-furnaces had all their five hot, scarlet mouths wide open as it passed, ruddying the mist, each a scorching leviathan with its dancing train of pigmy men. She did not look up at them.

Quite suddenly, as the train was plunging down into thick darkness again, she accepted as a sane and irrevocable truth all that the man in the chair had told her.

'It was the thing any of us might have done,' she mused.

That thought began a new attitude. In that odd, illogical, incomprehensible way women possess she found herself excusing him, defending him, even taking some proportion of his blame. Impulsively she pulled open her dress and saw the white, pointed breasts he had so often caressed, the scrap of amber on its silk string reposing between. And it seemed to her the honourable and decent thing to say: 'He spent all his money on me and made these debts until he could no longer go on making them without disgrace.' She recalled his presents, the peaches with a ring of bay-leaves, the ruby carnations, the black-and-silver ear-rings, the perfume, the editions of Chopin, the silver spoon. One by one they assumed an altogether disproportionate value and price in her mind. What they must have cost seemed to her unhappy, feminine intuition the cause of everything.

She suppressed with difficulty a desire to begin weeping, and covered over the breasts which she thought with a poignant ache he would not see again.

Her fortitude was lessening.

'Where has he gone? Why did he go like that? Why didn't he tell me?'

She blamed herself, excused him, and blamed herself more bitterly. She would have lent him the money.

This incredible act of his she saw suddenly as meaning for her a renewal of an existence without purpose or hope. She did not stop to compare herself with the figure of not many months before. The desires and thoughts of that restless, half-virgin time already seemed to her weak and pale. Only Andrew and her lovely, credulous passion for him seemed important and vital things.

She wept without a sound until the train braked to a standstill. Then she alighted and walked, with her head slightly averted, under the station lights. The mist was cold and her eyes smarted from weeping. Yet it had relieved her to weep and to think that as a gracious act towards him she would pay his debt.

She entered the street, the old dark houses closed in upon her, and the night was filled with the rustle of scentless wet lime-leaves. Constantly, not through any sense of a moral obligation, but because of the sweetness of an unfadable passion, she kept repeating that she would pay his debts for him, determinate and unshakable as ever.

'I shall pay, I shall pay,' she kept thinking, and the thought became a sort of defence for her.

Presently, however, she found herself before the green doors of the yard. It came as a shock to find herself there, and as though stupefied and troubled, she paused, went forward, then paused again. It was as if an awakening shout had gone through her mind: Why should she go in there again? Why should she ever return? From the depths of her being there rose a sense of revolt. Why had it eluded her, that thought? She had to go back; she had to face it all again; she was being driven under! 'I'm sure you feel it as much as we do,' flashed through her mind. The irony, the sense of something implacable thwarting her, of being withered into insignificance, were all unspeakable. Why should she be insignificant again, why endure an existence in

206 ·

which she would suffer? She grew excited, her tears starting at that sudden thought. Supposing she escaped? Supposing? She must escape! To go on hating Charles, lying, deceiving, wounding — why succumb to that, as if there were no other course, why prostrate herself unhappily? And unsteadily, impatiently, she searched for means of escape, trying to bring her mind to work upon the problem with tranquillity, yet at the same time longing for some force to solve it for her, and then, dejected, baffled, feeling little by little that perhaps it would never succeed.

Then, as on a previous occasion in early summer, her manner suddenly changed. Now, however, the mood was forced upon her and she became not indolent, not proud in bearing, but dispirited. She found herself accepting the fact of everything — the fact of her youth, the fact that something — she could not tell what — was draining her of courage, the fact that she felt powerless to prevent her life in that obscure street going on, indefinite, unrevolutionized, unalleviated except by the remembrance of things.

She felt herself grow cold, the mist trailing its shapeless pale skirts about her, but she did not move. Why did she not escape? Now for some reason she felt she would never escape, and almost it was as if she saw that life: the endless train of farmers, dealers and merchants tramping through the garden, the long winters, the boring, boring visitors to whom she would play the piano, Charles striving with his accounts, those distressing moments when she would remember Andrew; as if she already knew how even her petty world would go on comforting and hating itself, confiding and deceiving, whoring and loving, happy, tragic, amazed and troubled, even as she had been; as if she saw another summer already driving its flocks of linnets, thrushes, blackbirds and chaffinches into the trees again, the peaches burning to ripeness on the warm wall, the orange rose re-blooming, the wilderness of blue, white, scarlet and yellow petals flaunting itself towards the same decay; and lastly, as if she saw also herself little by little losing her fresh abundance of beauty, secretly and mutely nursing within herself the ache of an impassioned memory.

And slowly, as though unwillingly resigned to these things, she turned, mounted the steps to the black door, and then vanished suddenly into that obscurity from which she had once come.